Cutlass Wonders

{Being the First Tale in A Measure of Poe & Three Quarters}

Steven Mooney

Steven Mooney Books
Olympia, Washington

Cutlass Wonders

ISBN: 978-1-7345356-6-2
Library of Congress Control Number: 2020905113
Cover Art & Design by Jessica Bell Design
Published by Steven Mooney Books

This tale is dedicated to Dina,
Peter, Maureen, and Michael, and to the memory of
Doodlebug

Each story lives the humor of the ulcer while other maladies suffer to be heard.

– Randal Poe

Book One

Commencement Blues

It was to be a day of surprises that launched a season of them when through the privet he spied the Benz home early, ticking in the heat, tympanic to the yelling crescendos that scattered birds and boomed in the porte cochere and hit him full volume as he opened the door and even though he knew how to turn it off, this one was especially heated, and when he heard the word *college*, it caught him up.

"We must stand through thick and—"

"Thick as a brick—!"

"A free thinker, poets don't need algebra, he's—"

"A dolt, a wildcard, now this college denial—!" and something slammed the wall before his mother marched past trailing bourbon fumes while Randal lurked outside the den and observed his father fulminate and splutter while flying shards about their mountain land and that cutlass caught his ear before the senior Poe removed the sword from the mantle hooks and held it aloft. "Alas poor Yorick, the pen is mightier, so out with you then!" Randal watched his father march past with the stage prop and said Dad twice before their collision in the breezeway.

"You! 'How sharper than a serpent's tooth to have a witless whelp! Out, damned spot,'" and thrusting the instrument into the umbrella stand, the elder strode off.

Randal drew the cutlass from the bin as from a stone and unsheathed it in glittering light that anointed his riposte with his own quote of the Bard, addressing the cigar smoke that lingered like a shroud: "If the man were alive and would deny it, Zounds! I would make him eat a piece of my sword." The cutlass had been in the Poe family for generations, an heirloom vestige of a bygone epoch, and Randal seemed to have inherited it by default.

With the sword and a crumpled letter side by side on his desk, Randal learned he'd been denied admission to Carolingian College. His ascension to one of the South's storied institutions had been taken for granted; surely the only son of a noted playwright and professor would follow in his father's footsteps, or paw prints thought some, as the elder cast a simian resemblance in height and gait and patchy black beard. Yet the son was miscast in his father's eyes.

As he cleaned the scabbard with a pillowcase, disappointed by the rejection and stunned by the way it isolated him, the cripple unable to follow the Pied Piper, he was unable to accept that he'd be abandoned on the platform while everyone else would be getting on the train. What broken rules were these? College was a given, it was the standard follow through from senior year. Everybody was going. And had he heard correctly, he was to be kicked out of the house? He swished the air with the blade slashing at bureaucracy and parental stricture and then holding the sword aloft with both hands, he vowed that if he was to be made the goat of these corrupt, screwed up rules, then he'd rewrite them and shape them to his honor. He slid the sword under the bed before fanning the yellow pages.

"Darnell's Lock and Gun."

"Hey, I've heard y'all buy old weapons and so on."

"Got pawn, collectables, modern and antique: we do it all."

"Well, you need to check out this kickass blade."

"We close in a half-are, why don't you come on in tomorrow."

Randal wandered through the house like a ghost as he hatched a plan that didn't begin with getting kicked out of the house: he'd take whatever he could get for that blade, grab some cheap wheels and, well the plan ran out of gas at the city limits, but getting started was the thing, and the sword was the key. In the den he paused before the photograph of his triple-great grandfather brandishing the sword and noted again that he was a dead ringer for the guy, as though he couldn't see himself. He stared at his ancestor whose own life plans had been diverted by war; it really sucked about college; he assumed he would study English and history, the good stuff. In the dissipation of his dreams, he saw Fate in the role of Falstaff withholding the penny, and himself as Pistol; since the world is my oyster, I'll take the sword and crack a baker's dozen!

The next morning after his dad had left and he'd found his mother ensconced with an urn of Irish coffee, he took her wheels and drove downtown. Of their numerous cars he liked her Cadillac best except for a soured sense memory from the time the ape had gotten him in a headlock and wrestled him into the trunk for a refusal to go to church; and then just the car thing: his family was rich, and he deserved to have his own wheels, even classmates from the other side of the tracks were mobile. Randal stewed as he drove: anything he wanted to do, no matter what, Mister Big Shot Playwright was reading his mind like some black magic (he'd often pictured his father as the eighth dwarf in Snow White's train, cast from fairyland), using enchantment to write literature and screw him in every act and scene.

He parked in the side lot facing a crumbling brick wall where flag-shaped and faded patriotic colors read: *Darnell's Lock and Gun-Security is Our Business-Buy, Sell,*

Trade, and with his parcel he entered the store. It smelled of oiled steel and the floorboards creaked. On a pedestal sat a key-making machine beside a grandfather clock that stood sentry over centuries of gunnery and uniforms on hangers and on racks and rows of glass cases and vertical stacks along both walls displayed muskets and other vintage firearms. Mesmerized by the display, Randal stared as history winked.

"Can I hep you?" Randal turned to face a man with sandy brown hair pushed behind his ears, and wire-rim glasses.

"Lot of nice stuff there, much of it carried by our boys in the Civil War," said the man.

Randal stepped up and laid his bundle on the counter and unwrapped it. The tubby clerk peered.

"How much you give me for this blade?"

The man's reply was to lift the saber, turn it over in his hands, and then remove the blade from the scabbard and examine its designs. He slid the cutlass home and gently laid it on the glass.

"Where'd you get this?"

"It belonged to my grandfather."

"Mind my askin' who he was?"

"Shives Poe, he was a General."

"Shoot a mile! Your granddaddy was Gen'l Shives Poe?"

"Yep."

"Boy, you can't sell this sword. It's a gen-u-wine historic artifact. What I mean is, don't get me wrong, I'd love to buy it, but I ain't got ten thousand dollars!"

"Ten—are you shi-kidding me?"

"Listen, I could a said yeah, give you a hundred dollars and took it for myself, but you see I din't. Here's why, this sword belongs in a museum, or a battlefield, one." The clerk offered his hand.

"Elmer Butkins."

"Randal. What do you mean on a battlefield?"

"You heard of re-enactors?"

"I see I got a customer - you hole the fort."

Randal's eyes tumbled: Ten thousand bucks! He imagined a brass plate in the Smithsonian: 'From the Collection of Historian Randal Poe' as he hefted a musket from a rack, aimed down the barrel, and then held it at parade rest.

"Beautiful, ain't it?" said Elmer, back from selling a box of .22 longs. "That there's an 1860 Springfield. We carry many of 'em. You can't bring just any rifle. We make the same environment as a Civil War battle, and serious about it too."

"Sounds cool, what else y'all do?"

"Tell you what," said Elmer, "meet me Saturdee afternoon about five at Suds-n-Duds on Briar Boulevard, you know way it is? I gotta do my laundry, but I'll buy you a beer and tell ya about it."

"Well, okay, but I brought this sword down here because I need money pretty soon and, ah, my dad's a super tightwad."

"How much you need?"

"Well," and numbers danced as they often had.

"Tell you what, you let me display this sword, say a month, and I'll spot you a couple hundred. People will be askin' about it, word gets out. That'll mean business. I'll make money, and it'll be safe too, I guar-an-damn-tee-it."

Randal left the store with cash in his pocket and dollar signs in his eyes, salve to a busted spirit that over the next several days didn't keep a low profile so much as hone a stealth approach to home life, one he had unconsciously refined like an annual production with endless rehearsals for as long as he cared to look back.

But this day he looked forward as he pedaled his bike down Briar Boulevard.

A woman in an apron stared at sizzling meat as he entered Suds-n-Duds on the cafe side and took a seat at the bar, fronting a glass partition that separated the room from a laundro-mat.

"Hey, Donna, get my buddy a beer," called Elmer as he entered through a back door. They sat and watched the driers tumble. Exciting! Elmer turned up his bottle of Bud and slugged half. Randal again noted Elmer's belly, a tortoise shell under his shirt, and the same red suspenders as before, and they both watched Donna bend over burgers.

"There's nothing like a cole one, day like today."

Randal took a hit. His experience with drinking was tempered by stealing it from his dad.

"I was just out back workin' on my bike. Carb's a little funky."

"What kind of bike you got?"

"Harley, fifty-nine flat head," said Elmer as they went out, and Randal ogled the monster of a machine that seemed to be all engine topped with a gas tank, an oval seat and a smaller version behind it.

"Man, I love Harleys!"

"Chopped it myself and it's my pride and joy. Got me another back to the house, but this is my baby."

In awe, Randal reached for the handlebars.

"Hey! Can chew read?" cried Elmer, indicating a tiny sticker, and Randal, his nose an inch from the frame, read:

IF YOU VALUE YOUR LIFE
LIKE I VALUE MY BIKE
DON'T FUCK WITH IT

Rising, he stumbled and sprawled in gravel. Elmer handed Randal his beer.

"That's the reaction I'd like to get out of a good many people."

"Look, you gotta have a comma after bike; if-then clauses need a comma."

"You mean coma, what you get you mess with my bike. C'mon, I got to check my clothes," and they went back inside.

At the bar, Randal paged through a stack of mimeographed ads for re-enactments and after-battle and bivouac scenes given by the Third North Carolina Regiment, in addition to some newspaper clippings about the group.

"So, you try to make it real?"

"Historic accuracy, we call it."

"You're not concerned about somebody getting shot?"

"Hey now, we don't use live ammo. We did, the law be all over us. Besides, bunch of the guys are cops and troopers anyway, we legal inside and out." Randal pondered the historical accuracy of blank ammunition.

"Maybe I could play my grandfather."

"It don't work that way. It did, we'd have a hunnerd Robert E. Lees; there'd be more Stonewall Jacksons than your granddaddy's dogs. No sir, the Third puts a man where he's needed, and right now we're short litter bearers and muleteers."

Randal had pictured leading a charge, waving his sword like a lariat, or infantry attack, rows of shiny bayonets lined up straight as zippers, but ambulance driver? Elmer told him that his duties would be picking up dead off the field of battle. Where's the glory in that, he wondered, after all, they weren't really dead so how is *that* historically accurate? Suppose he collected some dead guys and put them in the ambulance, how long are they supposed to stay dead? What if you were dead out there and had to take a crap? What about jock itch? If you couldn't scratch that *would* kill you, he giggled, buzzed.

"So, you think you want to give it a whirl?" asked Elmer.

"I'll audition," he said around his tongue.

"Here's the dates when you should call. But hey, you come on by the store anytime, you hear?"

Randal gurgled as Elmer departed.

2

Dr. Titus Shell folded the newspaper and set it aside and pictured the columnist, Tarleton Ramseur, who'd attended many an opening at the museum, particularly the recent ceremony that inducted its new curator, and he smiled at the thought. Kept at the assistant level for so many years it was a godsend when a plastic Brontosaurus crushed his predecessor at an unveiling gone awry. Now in that title position at the North Carolina Museum of History, he cherished these moments when he could reflect or just kick back and relax with Ramseur's history column, and the current piece had detailed his museum's contribution to a National Geographic special on the state's role in reconstruction. The Civil War was never more than a moment away, it seemed. Only yesterday had another portal opened to him, a most surprising one as well. He'd received a call from a member of a Civil War Re-enactors Association, a group he'd helped fund from time to time. All he really knew about *Sergeant* Butkins was that he owned a local gun shop. But the conversation had excited him.

"You'll never guess what I got in my display case here."

"Newt Gingrich?"

"Haw haw! That's a good one."

"Get ready: I got Shives Poe's dress sword, the one give to him by Jeb Stuart!"

"Indeed!" had been Shell's initial reply. "How did you come across this gem?" He might have known better if he'd remembered how Butkins loved to ramble, especially when it concerned history. As the gunsmith warmed to his preamble, Shell reviewed what he knew about the General.

Shives Poe had had inherited a mercantile and dry goods store in Umstead Mills, then a rail stop crossroads southeast of Raleigh, and after twenty years had expanded it so far as to include a forge and smithy and a contract with the railroad, thus beginning a familial and financial relationship that would last well into the next century.

For one whose fortunes loomed so large, Poe's diminutive stature and low center of gravity attracted him to dogs and so he began breeding them as a pastime, one that bloomed when he established Poe Kennels, an endeavor that made him a slave owner; when he needed help to run the place, well, free labor was abundant. Revisionist history, if you buy it, has declared him to be more a frugal merchant than as one lacking in scruples, but an abomination no matter how one approached it. When North Carolina seceded from the Union, Poe was determined to become an officer but business kept him from the fuss to muster, and soon the hamlet seemed all but deserted. Poe then acted with a foresight that would establish him as a true hero of The Cause and guarantee him a place in history.

His dogs, already tough and trained, would be put to use, and he spent months working vigorously with his charges weeding out breeds and mutts but when satisfied that he'd done all he could his telegram to the governor applied for a Colonelcy and requested his Excellency's attendance at the review. Of course, the governor and other dignitaries thought Poe mad, but within a sultry hour, as the hounds performed in flawless drill, Poe's genius was realized and he was commissioned on the spot. The following day Colonel Poe marched away with the first detachment of what would grow to become Company K-Nine.

Poe's contribution to the first battle of Manassas, or Bull Run, has been written out of official histories (of the engagement). It had been impossible for the Union command to admit that a pack of dogs had turned their flank and driven them from the field in full view of Washington's polite society turned out in their finest livery. Conversely, General Thomas J. Jackson stated that when he gave the order to charge, Poe's troops had gotten underfoot and created a melee. Yes, the hounds charged the enemy, but they didn't fire a shot, he proclaimed, sucking a lemon. Nonetheless, partial credit for the victory was given to Poe in the form of his commission to brigadier general. Although the mix-up was disputed for years, once Stonewall was martyred, no one would have dared to place a dog before a god in the pantheon of that cause.

The battle of The Wilderness and its forest fires effectively ended the dogs as a combat unit, although they would be used extensively as messengers and on burial details throughout the war, but Poe had made his name and he served throughout the remainder of the conflict as a member of Ewell's staff, was wounded at Gettysburg and again at Cold Harbor, and ended the war sobbing at Appomattox Court House, Virginia. Five years after he returned home to his wife and family and mercantile, he was elected to the State House where he served until his death. His most prized possession was the sword presented to him by none other than General J.E.B. Stuart following the battle of Chancellorsville.

"What is the asking price?" said Shell, at last.

"He didn't specify, but I mentioned twenty-five."

"Hmm, well listen, Sergeant, promise me you won't accept any other offers until I get back to you, got that?" Now, as he sat in his office, he marveled at the memory; sometimes having an idiot in charge is a capital idea.

~ ~ ~

Several miles distant, Randal pined for the get-away money the sword might bring him, but until he could deal with that, he needed a place to stay even though his father hadn't acted. Randal was wary that his cloak of invisibility would wear off and his father might actually see him, and so spent little time at home, but one day on the stairs he ran into his mom.

"Son, I've tried to reason, and I've worn him down."

"What do you mean?"

"He's lined up a job for you with the railroad, and you can stay here—"

"I can't even be in the same county with—"

"one-hundred a month and kitchen privileges."

"Are you nuts?"

"Watch your tone, young man!"

"Ahh, Mom, I was going to write stuff, history, do English lit."

"Probably you should return that vulgar trophy to the den. And another thing, we've compromised, and I think it's the best."

"What is?"

"The attic."

"The attic?"

"It has its own stairway and kitchen entrance. It's very *backdoor*," she winked, and a peck on his cheek cut off the question, what about his room, and then she was off for a rose garden tea.

Randal ghosted on up but the remains of brunch and the newspaper caught his eye, and as he sat in the breakfast nook and scarfed crusted tarts, he thumbed through the sections until he found the page and the familiar column with its History Hotline at the bottom, and he used the landline to make the call. The voicemail caught him off guard and he stammered a message half-laughed as he aped the part of a belfry dweller in the castle of a crazed munchkin. Still in the groove, he balled up the sports page under his collar for the Quasimodo touch in the inspection of his turret when phone rang.

"Poe residence," he said, expecting one of his dad's cronies.

"Hello, may I please speak to Randal Poe? This is Tarleton Ramseur of the Raleigh News."

Whoa, that was fast! "Yes sir, speaking. I ah, called to see if you could determine the value of the sword I mentioned. It was presented to me by my dad as a reward for a sizzling SAT score."

"And you're here in Raleigh, is that correct?" Randal thought the voice fit the image of the noted columnist; the obese often sounded rotund.

"So, you're headed to Carolingian? Fine school; I went there, and your father teaches there, does he not?" Ramseur reviewed for a moment what he knew about the playwright.

Everett Poe, whose claim to fame was tethered by twenty some years with the Southern Pacific Railroad operating the scales used to weigh freight cars, an educated roughneck, had written a play that had since become an icon of Americana and a standard production on every stage in the nation, and if the oxymoronic platitude of the critics will stand, a modern classic. *Shadow Yards* had played so often on and off Broadway that it generated the hype of myth that led to a movie and then a remake. Poe's other plays have largely been ignored, but he was too rich to care, according to the gossip blogs. Ramseur spoke again.

"As to the blade, I'd really need to see it, examine it, before I could name a figure."

"That's okay, but there's something more: I'm really into history and I've written a lot for my high school paper. I'd like to know if you'd print the inside story; there's a lot of lore about this sword that you couldn't dig up in a library."

"Now there's a champion idea. I do support contributing writers, as you may know. I'll make you a deal. You bring that sabre here where I can ogle it, and I'll put you in print, how's that sound?" Randal tingled as they made arrangements.

Piloting the Caddy through traffic, Randal whistled. The day had been a smooth one. Borrowing his mom's car and the sword from Elmer had been cake, but it was the visit to the Ramseur home that was the icing; the house was as famous as its current occupants. Set in a grove of magnolias well back from the road, the pickets and gingerbread trim on the Greek revival had been hand turned for Governor Nelson Passwatter, renowned for his adolescent attempt to assassinate William Tecumseh Sherman with a garden tool. But before he could strike, GHQ drummer boys outflanked him and forced his surrender, though he was allowed to keep his rake. His act served a purpose greater than either the assailant or his intended victim: Union Army headquarters staff took up residence there while other mansions were ransacked or put to the torch. Since forever it had been listed in the state registry of historic places, and Tarleton Ramseur and his wife currently filled it with their bulk.

It turned out to be a day of surprises exceeded only by greater ones. First there was the journalist's wife, more rotund than her husband, but as light on her feet as a ballerina; then came the appraisal: Randal recalled the moment he'd almost blurted expletives. His astonishment had been assumed.

"Most people don't know the value of the stuff in their attics," said Ramseur.

Randal recalled his grandfather's trunk and the name stenciled on the lid, moldering in a corner.

"Here's a fine example, one you're tempted to rest your feet on. It's a bird's eye maple Drum table, over two hundred years old and worth a pretty penny. We found it in the cellar swathed in burlap."

Randal thought again of the trunk and what it may contain, and a plan began to form, one that took shape when Ramseur shook his hand and said: "I'll not only print this story you brought today, but any others you send. If they're written as well as this, you can become a regular contributing writer. Only one catch, you've got to remain in school and earn a B average or better. Those are my conditions. What do you say?"

Randal hoped that his mumbled response was appropriate to the committed lie. Later that day when he dropped off the sword, Elmer told him to return the following day, as they had matters to discuss.

The next morning Randal found both cars gone and couldn't locate the keys to the other two and had to take his mountain bike to the gun shop, and as he scooted through the hedge, he knew that the attic just wasn't going to do. Elmer was locking up as he arrived.

"Eyeballed your measurements, and nothing here's gonna fit you. But I got a load more out to the house.

You can ride with me since my bike moves faster than yours, haw haw."

Randal eyeballed the passenger's seat, about the size of his shoe.

"You just don't squirm around, and lean when I lean, you'll be alright." And all right he had been from the moment Elmer launched into the air and came down on the starter pedal. As the bike throbbed to life Randal arranged himself on the pad over the rear bumper and was then so entranced with the ride, the cathedral ceiling of trees rolling overhead, the next thing he knew he was climbing all rubbery off the bike.

"That's the vibe," said a grinning Elmer, tossing his helmet on the grass. "Show you somethin." And he led the way around the side of the house to a detached garage and there in the middle of the floor sat another hog, this one with a yellow teardrop tank and a purple frame. Randal went numb.

"This used to be my baby. One we rode is older, an antique, really. This bike's only, less see, sixteen years old." He attempted to start it by a series of frantic leaps.

"You know why they call it a Harley?"

"Because it *Harley* ever starts," trumpeted Randal, proud of his insider knowledge. They returned to the house, a white A-frame with green shutters loose on punky hinges. Randal expected a clutter of motorcycle parts and beer cans but was surprised to see furniture that reminded him of the Ramseur's, knurled, every room was stately.

"House belonged to my granddaddy Darnell. They took care a me and my brother when our folks got killed. Store was my daddy's. Buster split, that's my brother, so it's all mine."

"How'd they die, you parents?"

"It was a head-on collision right out there on 401, some shitfaced farmer on his way to hell, killed 'em all."

"I don't have parents, either," said Randal.

Elmer studied him a moment. "You mean y'all don't get *along*, that's one long-ass road from never again."

Randal remembered the day their last maid hit the highway (much the way they all had) and the electric sheen of her face as she went with a dignified silence out the door, as though her tears had merged with sweat to cool her blood that had been scorched by the bourbon furnace of Matilda's wrath and of Everett's biliary weathervane. He'd often laid awake as their screed echoed through the old house like the creaking of a schooner in a gale, and perhaps as often had wondered what his parents saw in each other in the first instance of their meeting; he couldn't for the life of him imagine that summer romance, dating, enjoying each other's estival laughter, light as butterflies. In photos she was a dark stunner, as yet unpickled and he, though a younger version of the current satyr, wore a smile Randal had otherwise never seen.

"Mostly I'm not a person to them."

"Well, enough about that; let me show you the stuff here," and they entered a room that resembled a museum display: uniforms and hats and caps and sashes and boots in many sizes were stacked in assorted piles.

"Here, put these on. I'm get us a couple beers." Randal changed into pants that were scratchy and too big in the seat, but when he looked in the mirror it was as though he saw himself for the first time, a wide grin in a sunny brown face.

"Got a belt?"

"Suspenders, more likely; it's got to be period perfect." After fiddling and adjusting he saw the General dissolve and in his stead a curly black-haired rebel soldier stared back, a bit astonished, as though seeing himself for the first time, but he knew the daredevil grin that drew Audrey but otherwise lay dormant was about to emerge like a chrysalis. Later, pedaling his bike home he inserted the purple-yellow hog into his plan and giggled when it seemed to fit into his itching to roll: old Ev is going to pop an eyeball!

3

Titus Shell had rammed through the requisition, waiving formalities while crowing to colleagues about the impending purchase, and though he would need to see it to be sure, if it was indeed the genuine article it could be the key to early retirement, and as he picked up the phone, he daydreamed of sailing down to the Yucatan and buying a hacienda on the beach.

"Lo, Darnell's Lock and Gun."

"Sergeant Butkins, Titus Shell here."

"Hey, listen, had a lot a people in here on account of it, yes sir, they been lining up like it's the State Fair."

Shell thought: Good, there's been no one. "Well, I hope you've kept your counsel."

"My word is good as gold, sir."

"I would like to arrange a time to visit. It is vital to determine if it's the real McCoy before any appraisal can be made. I'm sure you understand."

"Well, this afternoon's as good a time as any."

"I'll be there at three."

That afternoon, with nothing to do but wonder about money, Randal entered the gun shop but there didn't seem to be anyone in attendance and an impulse found him behind the counter at the register, along with a daydream: *Randal's Lock and Gun, may I help you? A faceless tease in a yellow string bikini pointed at him and said: I want that one.* He wondered at the image of Audrey, faded already to a curvaceous fantasy devoid of the personality that had at first found him vital but then mediocre, yet fantasy had been her game, ever teasing him to slathering before wiggling away, a desperate ideal for sure, but then the moment shattered as he spied Elmer crossing the street and fearing a breach of faith, he vaulted the counter and landed in the full uniform rack, concealing himself in duds. It was a routine long perfected by eavesdropping on his parents, lounging amid the gabardine in their walk-in closet. He would pop out and surprise the gunsmith as he wolfed his lunch: two Big Macs with two large fries salted like German pretzels, with a foghorn belch allowed for passage, but Randal, suffused in aromatic canvas and wool, became a witness to his destiny as a customer entered.

"Sergeant." Shell straightened his tie and stepped up to the counter.

"There she sets."

"Let's have a look, shall we?" Elmer slid the panel on the display case and withdrew the cutlass. Shell looked it over as Elmer watched him and Randal watched them both. Shell drew the sword from the scabbard and gently laid the sleeve on the glass. The graceful curve of the burnished steel blade was engraved with hunting scenes of men and horses and dogs, the figures finely wrought on the polished blade of the foible and the forte between the true edge and the false edge; a vine meshed foliate swirl entwined the gilt letters C.S.A. and along the obverse ricasso was the gilded script: *Presented to General Shives Poe by General J.E.B. Stuart, Aug. 1863.* The scabbard was brass mounted with gold carrying rings and a silver drag. A slight whistle leaked from Shell as he noted the script fronting the hilt, for he knew he was among the few to have ever held this sword, and that list was topped by Stuart himself.

"You've seen the name, I take it," he said, finding his mouth was dry.

"Yes siree! It's a real piece of history."

"There's not another one like it."

"I learned that too," said Elmer.

"Oh?" Shell eyed him as he slid the blade home.

"Yeah, I figgered I better check, so I went on the big web."

"The World Wide Web, you mean?" Shell felt as though he was at the edge of a great precipice, one breathless step from—

"Yep, and to think I'd a let it go for twenty-five thousand when it was worth twice as much."

Shell almost blurted 'a lot more than that' before he choked it, and Randal, fixated in a mesh of tunics where chevrons flanked him like extra sets of eyebrows, also caught himself, the figure being lower than Ramseur's quote.

"Well, that may be somewhat inflated," said Shell, "listings such as you've seen always offer the highest price, it gives them room to maneuver in barter and trade." He went on to explicate the antiques and artifacts market using a deft display of insider knowledge peppered with buzzwords; he needed to re-establish control, one that had momentarily slipped away.

Elmer only half-listened to the prattle and parlance; he knew he had his man between a rock and another rock and fancy words were just hot air and besides, he didn't like being talked down to. When his folks were killed, and somebody had to help gramps run the store, he'd left college. Shoot, if anybody was stupid it was his brother. Buster often had both feet in the same shoe. While Elmer traipsed off into kinship memories, Randal realized he was on the brink of something big. It was so big that it blotted out his ability to see how big it really was, and he was itching to free himself from his grotto of jerkins. His legs were numb, but he wanted to run, just run and run and leap into a river and float away.

During his spiel Shell had done some calculations: a rare talent, he knew, and clearly an asset when dealing with antiques and the people who kept them, often unaware of their value. He concluded his lecture with an offer. Elmer chuckled.

"No, sir, I believe this sword will fetch the full fifty, if not more."

As Shell left the shop, he knew he had a fight on his hands. Elmer locked the register and strolled with a magazine into the back bathroom. Randal quietly slipped out of the store and headed home.

The house seemed deserted, but as he made his way through the rooms, he caught faint grunts and huffs and knew what they were up to. In the study he Googled a list of antique dealers; he certainly wasn't going to let Elmer take advantage of him. In the letter he then wrote was contained as much of Shell's description as he could remember, and he quoted the sword at a higher price than Elmer and Shell combined, and well over that of Ramseur. Then, fishing the keys out of his mom's purse he braced for that car's pine sap deodorizer and drove downtown to the Post Office. Shell's remark about starting high seemed to make sense, as did the thought that if the state had really wanted the sword, they wouldn't have sent a skinflint. His next stop was to see Elmer.

"Hey bud, sup?"

"I need the sword, if you don't mind."

"Been meaning to mention that," said Elmer. "We had us an offer I think you should consider: seven thousand dollars!"

Randal simmered but held his tongue. "Well, I'll think about it, but I got to take a pic of it with my—"

"Folks, I bet, a proud moment for you," said Elmer, rescuing the boy from the tangle of impromptu subterfuge.

"Next Saturday still on?"

"Coming on like a hot babe; you need to be out to my place no later than six thirty, and you got no wheels. Tell you what, sell that blade to my contact and buy ya self some."

"Why don't you sell me that yellow Harley?"

"Now there's a thought."

Randal left the store and made his way back home tingling: just think, first I take part in the 17th battle of Chickamauga, and then I'll get that chopper, and then a new home!

Rummaging in his new digs in preparation for the battle, he recalled the day his mother and grandmother enlisted his help into arranging generations of family stuff up here under the eaves, color-coded in a notebook hung on a nail. With relish he recalled that he could locate the pencil that the Toad from Hell had used to write that play and grind it down to a nub. He checked the trunks against the notebook, found the right one, and raised the lid.

A tray set in notches held musty leather-bound books. He lifted it out and beneath that were piles of satchels and these too he set on the floor. From a plastic garment bag, he removed a gray uniform coat with amber piping and epaulets like shriveled sunflowers and held it up to the light. You're looking a little thin there, Shives; but hey, you *are* a hundred and fifty years old. Then something caught his eye: a pair of cracked and rotting leather boots placed lengthwise on the bottom of the trunk. The boot tops were inches apart but between them there gleamed a silver band. He slid the boots off and exposed a sword. Holy shit, there're two of them. He drew the blade from the scabbard and carried it over to the light, but there were no engravings at all, otherwise it looked much the same. Holding it aloft he realized those weren't hunting scenes on the other sword, but a depiction of his ancestor with the Canine Company, and it hit him how he could double his earnings if he played it right, even if doing so would be wrong; but who was the wronged one here, whose history of abuse, of neglect, was a recurring family conflict with a north and a south as symbols of love and denial? A north and south… where did *that* come from, he wondered, as he laid the sword aside and lifted up a heavy pistol. It resembled others he'd seen at Darnell's except this one had gilded letters stamped in the grips: S.P. C.S.A. and he brought it up in both hands and sighted down the barrel before opening a few more bags hoping to find a forage cap, but soon reasoned that generals didn't forage. Then, with the pistol and the sword wrapped in a bed sheet, on his way out of the garret he picked up his varsity football helmet.

Back in his room he laid the sword behind the other one and recalled the wooden display case that his former scout troop used to hold its jamboree awards, and where they hid the key to the hut. It would work. Then, as he put on the helmet, his thoughts shifted to playing ball once he'd gotten to college and playing the field too where there'd be hundreds of authentic young women, not Audrey types. But he'd been denied *the given* to almost everyone he knew and sensed that he'd crossed a meridian, some road less taken, but was cheered by the thought that if Robert Frost had ridden a motorcycle, it would have turned out differently, as it would for him: the motorcycle thing could work: he saw himself riding it away from Umstead Mills and the thought was a salve to his spirit, and he took the helmet down to the basement tool bench to pry off the faceguard. Coming up the stairs he bumped into his mom.

"Hon, your father and I will be gone this weekend, so you'll have the place to yourself. Just remember to lock the door when you go out."

"Okay. Can I use your car?"

Matilda considered her husband's response to this old question, and it didn't help. She knew her son was lost, and that he had no idea what to do with himself once college was ruled out. They'd gotten tutors to help, the best that money could buy, but it hadn't been enough. She felt hapless to measure the sum of his despair, and besides they were going to be late if they didn't leave soon, so she resorted to pocketbook wisdom.

"Here: I had a spare set made," she said, and also handed him two fifties.

The elders had been gone several hours when Randal opened a letter from the day's mail.

Dear Sir,

I am responding to your letter as concerns your grandfather's sword. I am a private collector of Civil War artifacts, and in my collection, I possess a letter from General Stuart in which he describes in considerable detail the gift he made to General Poe. That I would now have an opportunity to purchase that cutlass excites me to no end. I am prepared to pay the price offered, in cash, in order to secure its purchase. My phone number is above on the letterhead. Please call at your earliest convenience.

Sincerely,

Leutius D. McKee

"That was fleet," Randal said aloud as he lurched for the phone.

"Go ahead."

"Hey! This is Randal Poe. I just got your letter."

"Have you made a sale as yet?"

"Well, I have feelers out, but you're the first to ask about it," said Randal.

"Son, I am very serious about this. If there have been other offers, I need to know."

"You have my word."

"Are you in Raleigh now?"

"Well, it's Umstead Mills, old Raleigh, inside the beltway."

"How does this evening sound? I can be there by five, six at the latest."

"Yeah, that's great!"

"Any dealers there I should be concerned about?"

"Nah, there's no one that wants it, *yet.*"

"I'll see you in a few hours then."

Randal hung up the phone and yelled, picturing the chopper in Elmer's garage. He gathered his stuff and laid the sword and scabbard side by side on a blue velvet comforter and took a dozen photographs with his father's Nikon.

~ ~ ~

Leaning back in his chair, McKee again scanned General Stuart's letter framed in laminate Confederate banknotes he his brother had once won at the State Fair, thus kindling his passion for the era, one their father helped to broaden through leisure knowledge of period antiques, and now supported by golf courses and hog farms in three states. By the time L.D. graduated from college, he had an enviable collection of regalia: from brass buttons and minie balls, to written orders by officers both famous and obscure.

After landing and securing the plane at RDU he called Randal for directions, playing with him to see how well he matched with Google Maps. Imagine that, as he drove the rental, he pondered that the kid doesn't even know how to give directions in his own town; but a lot of people are like that. You live in a place your entire life but never notice much about it. He'd gone to school at State and had a pretty good idea the Poe residence was located near Oakwood but driving through it he noted that the old sights just weren't the same.

L. D. rang the bell and was greeted by a kid of about twenty who, following his inspection of the blade and their transaction, couldn't stop shaking his hand. Following his taxi and take off on his return flight to Charlotte, he again reflected on the interludes of *Time.* The Poe kid had spoken of re-enactors and their take on historical accuracy, but people, places were different then, nothing like it is now; even the poorest Deep South isn't free of pesticides, and I ought to know, he chuckled. But it had been a great day. On the floor of the cockpit lay the latest addition to his horde, an immaculate weapon once hefted by General James Ewell Brown Stuart!

His enthusiasm for money well spent, however, was tempered the following day as he and his chief number cruncher strolled through a pine grove. Dressed for tennis, McKee didn't understand how on a dog day like this the man could wear a suit. He didn't require formal dress of any employee, but then he realized he hadn't been paying attention.

"So ultimately, this hog farm is likely to become a liability. There's no writing on the wall, so to speak, but it would be a good gamble to get out before there's a stampede."

"So, in summary, the main points are?"

"Sir, we are on the verge of going into the red at Hogville: to make the necessary alterations and to overhaul the system, well, the equipment upgrade is simply going to cost more than the operation is worth."

"Just give me a number." Then L.D. felt his ears jump.

"Harold Christmas! I see your point," and L.D. then reflected on the favors owed by a couple Senators, long overdue, time to pay up or shut up.

"Needless to say, a quick sale avoids everything," said the florid executive.

"Thank you, Arthur, I'll give this some thought."

"One other thing, sir. Insider whispers indicate that Doodle-Do Farms is about to go on the market, lock, stock, and eggs. What I see is McKee Farms moving pigs out and chickens in, a fell swoop but for one catch."

"What's that?"

"Those hog farmers, sir."

"Well, you leave that to me…Doodle-Do, eh?"

Following an hour of tennis with his wife, he settled in his study and made some phone calls, and so began to see how this state of affairs fit into his game plan. He'd been toying with the idea of getting out of hogs, concentrating more on feed with one eye cocked toward chickens. Soon after, he typed a memo on Hogville's gray foolscap and posted it for delivery.

5

Randal couldn't stop counting the bills as the tops on bottle after bottle of his dad's beer popped amid flung handfuls of cash and he danced in a rain of fluttering money. Holy mother of God, a hundred thousand bucks! I'm rich, and I'll have wheels by the time that rock ape returns from Hilton Head! He rolled bills into cylinders and sang through them, made paper airplanes and sailed them and hopped and hooted and howled and at dawn awoke on the floor sprawled across that odd green blanket and after a hair of the dog and a bagel he remembered a loose floorboard under the General's trunk and hid his money before raiding the fridge for freezer bags of food to go, and he and Elmer were soon on their way to the battle.

"This is a real stretch for me, you understand," said Elmer.

"What do you mean?"

"Riding *in* something instead of on it; I'll probably catch hell them boys see me. What is it anyhow?"

"Cadillac," said Randal.

Elmer nodded and whistled. They rolled on down the road as Randal thought of the Moped his dad had offered when he'd turned sixteen, baiting him, and the promised fishing trips that never came to pass, the birthday presents and allowances denied that were seemingly based on vague transgressions, but he switched off then and drummed the steering wheel to the beat of Metallica while beside him Elmer played with the push-button windows but then punched off the tunes.

"What the hell?"

"You got to practice makin' the Rebel yell. Go ahead on, try it out." Randal yelped.

"Go higher." Randal went again.

"You're too low; it's gotta be a whole lot higher. Listen a me: AIEEEEEYAIEEEEY," screeched Elmer, like a rooster from hell.

"Damn! That's something else!"

"Took me a while too, couldn't get it until one day Buster and me was fighting and I side kicked him but he caught me half way right in the balls."

Randal imagined ranks of soldiers kicking each other; an officer on a bandstand waving a baton and as he drove, and he reflected on the connection between yelling and language: 'the only way dad ever talks to me.'

"Nice ride you got here, son, this is tits."

On their arrival, Randal imagined the two armies stumbling into each other through these pine thickets, pickets out before them their only guide, but this day placards in blue and grey announced each regimental bivouac. Randal found his unit and was soon in action.

Private Poe strolled among the fallen soldiers, pulling and tugging at the uniform that chafed him in a sauna of wool, his shirt smelled like it hadn't been washed since the original battle, and he was dying of thirst. Among the elected dead he noted a man who rolled periodically to scratch, so he sauntered on over and saw that like many of the others he was smeared with ketchup and flies.

"What, you get shot in the butt?"

"Shut the fuck up."

"I reckon I'd twitch too I had to lie there in the sun all day."

"It ain't all day shit for brains," said the grey-clad man as he plowed his ass.

"Well, I'm like a litter bearer, so I can help you out."

"You're that cherry came in with old Butkiss."

"Randal Poe," and he offered a hand to the fallen comrade.

"You not sposed to act like we're on a street corner, this here's a battle and we're in the same regiment," and he rolled over again. "I got rhoids something fierce," said the man, and Randal was relieved they hadn't pressed the flesh as he stood there sweltering and the sounds of battle rose and fell like the breath of a raging ogre.

"Here, put these in yer wagon," said the man, raking to Randal a squad of empty ketchup bottles of the size favored by the leisure industry.

"So, this is what, blood?"

"Wounded you carry them packets what come with french fries but shot dead or blown up you get these. E.E. Terrell, you call me Eddie."

"What's the other E stand for?"

"Ernest, and I ever hear you say it I'll kick your ass into next week."

"I've got something might help you," said Randal, and he loped off with the condiment bottles. Returning, he offered his canteen.

Terrell elevated an elbow and drank, squinted, and swigged again.

"Damn, boy, you're alright. Colonel ever hears about this your ass is grass."

"There's more in the wagon."

They straggled off, Terrell limping for effect.

At the wagon, a Conestoga loan, Randal pulled hot Budweisers from his grandfather's boots.

"Where you get them," said Terrell.

"Grandfather."

"A hero, am I right?"

"Are you from Carolina?"

"Who's asking?"

"But from the south, right?" asked Randal.

"Naw, it's Wis-fuckin-sconsin," said Terrell, hitting his beer. "I'm down here all the time."

They climbed from the wagon to see reenactors streaming out of the woods and heading across the field: the battle had concluded according to schedule, and Randal noted how nicely the timetable allotments routed the warriors toward the historically accurate parking lot.

"C'mon, it's breaking up," and they joined in pulling the wagon over the ground they'd traversed that morning. Then Eddie led him down a row of cars and popped the trunk on a Camaro. Randal stood slack jawed as he surveyed an arsenal that included M-16s and hand grenades and what may have been a bazooka.

"Got flak vests and walkie-talkie's too," claimed Eddie.

"You run a gun store like Elmer, huh?"

"Them Butt kiss brothers about as worthless as Near Beer. Got a Militia; the recruiting office is always open. Call, you want to defend your country," said Terrell, removing his uniform.

"Like that one out in Idaho, or Nebraska," said Randal, recalling how geography and all the sciences had eluded him, as had the demand of math to solve for the Roman alphabet.

"Those boys itching to get shot," stated Eddie, "like that one down Texas thought he was Jesus; did they wait for him to drag a cross through Waco? No sir, they cooked his ass quicker than snot catches flies."

"Yeah, I watched it on TV with my dad," said Randal, reliving the stench of his father's cologne and the running commentary on how they were getting their just deserves. Eddie placed an embossed card in his hand, said to stay in touch, and burned rubber.

Randal heard his name and turned to see Elmer with an older man whose beard had become unglued below an ear and flapped like a banner.

"Randal, this here's our own Stonewall Jackson. Duke, this is my friend that writes for the Raleigh News, just joined the regiment and he's looking for a scoop interview with a big shot." Randal glared; they had discussed no such thing.

"I'll be happy to oblige, fire away," said the flapping beard as Elmer handed over a pad and pen.

"Well, ah, would you tell me your name and what you do, for a living I mean."

"Surely, I am—hang on a minute, I do not want my name in the newspapers."

"What do you do, then?"

"Why not go with Stonewall Jackson, folks will get a kick out of it," said Elmer.

"Good idea," said the flapping beard, as Randal rolled his eyes; this has got to be the dumbest thing.

"Alright, *Stonewall*, what do you do for a living when you're not otherwise dead?"

The beard turned to Elmer. "Our last comedian spent his battles peeling potatoes."

"But he wasn't no journalist. This here's different."

Randal then recognized an anomaly, but he'd hold it for a while. "Sir, you may remain as anonymous as you wish, but you realize, I suppose, that any mention of your livelihood will likely identify you to friends and family."

"Okay, we'll just say that I am associated with—that won't give anything away because we have many people punching the clock every day at Heads Held High, in Greensboro."

"What is that, exactly?"

"Wigs."

"Wigs? You sell wigs."

"We have wigs for all shapes and sizes for women and men, as well as for children and for some pets."

Randal stopped writing. "I don't believe that I've ever encountered a bald child," he said, "much less a poodle with a pompadour."

"Now listen…" but the beard took flight and Stonewall cupped his elbow splaying fingers against the runaway and Randal noticed the delinquent auburn whiskers mismatched the burnt sienna just visible under the gray hat, and he'd had about enough.

"You're wearing a wig today, from your product line?"

"And what if I am?" The swiveled hip made Randal uneasy.

"Well, it's not exactly historically accurate, and while we're at it, and please correct me if I'm wrong, but Jackson wasn't present at Chickamauga."

"Well, you certainly are wrong, private, and let me say if you wish to advance in this regiment, you'll mind your p's and q's."

"Isn't it true he was already dead, shot at Chancellorsville several months previous to the slaughter here?"

"Come along Sergeant Butkins; this interview is finished," and an unwitting Elmer was seized by the arm and hauled away by his commanding officer, out of earshot of the rejoinder on the North Carolina volley that had toppled Stonewall from his horse.

After the battle and the long drive back, the contentious interview was skirted in the beery conversation that went late into the night. The following morning Elmer and Randal sat on the front steps, the morning hot and hazy and buzzing with tree frogs in the maples and oaks in the yard that shaded the house and kept the porch cool. A mockingbird sang its hit parade somewhere near, and cars passed, their occupants dressed for church. Randal had always loved the approach of deep summer, especially in the woods where you could breathe its aroma of rot and ripe, the going and the gone, and in a single breath a measure of time. He sipped his beer as Elmer flicked pebbles at a caterpillar inching up a dogwood.

"That was some battle, yes sireee," said Elmer.

"Well, I missed most of it, and so did those dead guys." They'd stayed up late discussing it, and now they were at it again.

"That'll change, you get seniority."

Randal watched the caterpillar but saw a trunk full of ammo.

"You ever run into this guy, Eddie Terrell?"

Elmer hung his head, and then went inside and returned and handed Randal a photograph. In it were two men, arm in arm, who stood by chopped motorcycles. Eddie was on the left. The other man resembled Elmer but for a flat top haircut and arms marbled with bottle-green tattoos. At the edge of the picture a woman in jeans and a tank drank from an upturned bottle of booze. Elmer snatched back the picture.

"This here's two years ago. You see Terrell. That other one's my brother, Buster, and they're best friends."

"Who's the girl?" asked Randal.

"You don't wanna know."

They sat awhile. A pebble scored a direct hit and the caterpillar tumbled.

"That there's Leslie."

"Wow, a beauty and a half," said Randal.

"Aw, damn it to hell," said Elmer, "we were tight."

"I guess she's not around any—"

"That bitch Terrell ran off with her, and Buster he knew she was side-saddle and he never tole me." Elmer rose and began pacing, his belly leading the way.

"They all three ran off."

"Eddie's from the mountains," said Randal, trying to be helpful.

"Last I heard that's where they are, but Buster, he don't stick long to one place."

Randal drained his beer and pictured the stacked cases of motorcycles he could get for a hundred grand; it staggered him.

"Buster and me we run the store after Granddaddy got too old. It's a lot a work, I got to tell you, but then one day he just left. We were real close, from when we was knee high to a Nehi. And then of a sudden, I didn't know him. It's weird."

"So, what's up with this militia?" asked Randal.

Elmer stopped pacing and scowled. "Those boys up there don't know jack shit about the Bill of Rights," and he stormed inside and slammed the door. Randal chewed on that a while and then left and drove down the shade-mottled roads, and as dappled sunlight splashed the windows, further tracings of the attic scheme began to gel.

The following day as he went over the escape plan, he felt weightless and understood it as a symptom of freedom that was just heartbeats away, and he was pleased that he had gotten his handiwork done before the battle: the sheathed sword resting on velvet under sealed glass. As he polished the purloined display case, his well-stocked bookshelf caught his eye. Usually, he went milky when he regarded this treasure, his English and history books and the hard work of a dedicated writer, but instead of a Byron or a Hemingway, all he saw was that journalism was his ticket, and history was history; his old plans now about as real as the faux Chickamauga. With that driving him he bungied his package to the handlebars of his bike and pedaling sedately, delivered it to the gun store. Elmer sat behind the counter, his mouth hanging open.

"This is how it's going to be," said Randal. "I appreciate your getting me into the regiment and Chickamauga and all, but you were screwing me on the sword."

Elmer's eyes dropped to the wood and glass box and the accompanying color photograph, studied it, and he shook his head. "Didn't really know how much it was worth. Look, good buddy, I need to make a buck, right?"

"Elmer, I'm going to cut you in, give you a percentage. But don't screw me again, it's petty bullshit."

Elmer almost sang: how about a burger and a Coke, on me?

When he was gone, Randal shouldered one of the muskets and thought: you don't need a gun to make a killing, all you need is money. When he returned later that day, he tucked a wad of it in Elmer's shirt pocket after he'd climbed off the Harley, and then they stood around the garage discussing Randal's new wheels. Then with a howl, he leaped on the starter pedal and rumbled out of the yard and rode the bike in second gear, not fast and not slow, savoring it, revving the throttle as he throbbed along the tree-lined streets, enjoying the wind on him and the arched branches overhead. Then, from a block away he opened it up and roared into the driveway and leaned the bike on its side stand. As he removed the German army coalscuttle Elmer had given him in place of the football helmet, his father came charging out of the house like a rodeo bull.

"What the hell is this!" From the perch of his new motorcycle boots that gave him a height advantage, Randal knew power for the first time in his life.

"S' up, dad?"

"I asked you a goddam question. What do you think this is?"

"It's a motorcycle."

"Don't smart ass me, boy," fired Everett, his face a crimson wrap around the stogy in his jaw.

Randal smiled and patted the gas tank. "My new wheels: just bought it."

Livid, Poe walked around the bike like a drill instructor inspecting a pissant recruit. He'd always hated motorcycles because he was too short of stature to straddle one and recalled with distaste the members of his Southern Pacific work gang that had ridden bikes like this, roaring by with their girlfriends wrapped around them.

"You get this piece of junk out of my yard."

"It's not in the yard, it's in the driveway," spoke the giddy son. Everett stepped up and thumped a finger on the boy's chest.

"I am not going to say this again, shit-hook. I don't know who the *hell* you think you are, but you're not going to trash my property" he bellowed, and stormed back inside.

Chanting curses, Randal wheeled the bike to the curb. There! you don't own the street, do you? He headed for the backdoor.

~ ~ ~

Years back, Titus Shell had seen a Broadway production of *Shadow Yards* but until that day he had made no familial connection between the famed playwright and the General, whose sword he'd purchased for the state, though it would technically be his long enough to strike a knockout blow of one-upmanship with his brother, to whom he'd been trying to measure up most of his life. He had planned a devilish surprise, yet it was only after waltzing through the museum with his purchase, crowing to anyone in earshot, that back in his office he had the devil of a surprise of his own when he opened the box and unsheathed the blade: he had been duped! He slid the naked blade back home but then drew it again to see what, that it had been but a dream, that the miniature figures had resumed their positions? It just hadn't crossed his mind to double check the contents of the display case against the photograph when he'd bought it at the gun shop, and now he wrung his hands and burned in anger and shame: what a fool he had been! And what a fool he would seem if this got out—and how could it not; there were wolves on his staff who thought his rise premature and who would relish a chance to eat his lunch, but as his anger burned away it became a blue flame of fear. 'Think!' First, he locked the sword away and stashed the photo in his desk. Sitting behind it he got himself under control with his pipe and tobacco and concentrated not on the box he was in but where the opening may be found to get him out, and with pipe lit he puffed up a plan and then covered the ground, checking loose ends and their pesky consequences, and found himself spinning as he went over the same points, inept at deception, but excited nonetheless.

The next morning, he visited a brazing company, whose owner turned out scrollwork and other forms of metal brocade that *invested in the old South the vigor of the new.* Shell fanned the brochure as the foreman sized up time, labor, and material as he appraised the photo of General Poe's sword, as well as his customer.

"Is this finery possible to replicate?" said an impatient Shell.

"Well sir, the real question ought to be why all the interest in this thing."

"What int—what do you mean?"

"Couple weeks back could a got you a two-fer."

"This sword, this one right here?"

"Shoot, the more of 'em you make, the lower the cost. Customer comes out ahead how it works, but that other fellow didn't want but one, either."

Shell fumbled for answers. "Tell me, what did he look like?"

"Might be you know him, work you a deal, that it?"

"That about sizes it up."

"Well, he looked like that actor what's his name, guy with the jaw, but hang on, I got his card," said the foreman, rooting about on his desk. "That level of engraving, a young guy here fresh out of design school got this fellow a pretty good likeness.

"Here it is," he said, handing Shell the business card.

"Sonofabitch!" It was a seemingly innocuous detail for all the foibles that would issue from it.

Book Two

Welcome to Hogville

The letters mailed out by McKee Farms were received in turn with concern, astonishment, and delight. They stated that the farms at Bessboro would be contracted either collectively or individually, and that the current tenants would be given the first bid, in an arrangement known as contract farming. A corporate owner (in this case the nonincorporated McKee Farms) paid a nominal fee to the farmers to raise the hogs, and who would be financially responsible for the operation of the farm and the upkeep of the barns, pens, and equipment, as well as for any mishaps. Once the farmers had paid the mortgage, they could earn big money. It was a sweet deal, wasn't it?

Such a set-up is common in large-scale livestock production in spite of the risks; a loophole allowed the owner to back out at any time, but there was no such leeway for the farmers who often had to borrow money for the upkeep or expansion of the metal barns with their effluvium chutes and open-air waste pits commonly called lagoons. Here, the tenants, members of an extended family, raised some of those points.

The Honeycutts had been on the land for many generations and therefore a sharecropping ascendancy was assumed. They had long wanted to put the family name on a banner that proclaimed their rightful ownership of thousands of smiling pigs, when they could then petition the legislature to have Hogville, as it was affectionately known, placed on the map, even though Bessboro was but a crossroads, a wide spot in the road that had grown up around three hog farms. Lore centered on Bess, the sow that begat the original breed, the first generation of a dynasty with an unequaled longevity, the Habsburgs of hogs.

From the beginning, scattered shacks had grown through the years to a village of them on the hardscrabble farm and the turn of a new century brought a general store, soon to add a lone pump filling station.

Now, embracing a new century, Bessboro had a couple dozen houses and a converted barn movie theatre that doubled as post office and bus stop, and next-door sat the dilapidated Shoat Motel and cafe. The current residents, first, second, and third generation Honeycutts, believed it was only a matter of time before they had them a mall. Even so, they couldn't imagine another life. Framed on a livingroom wall were an ancestor's words: *You can take the farmer out of the hog, but you can't take the hog out of the farmer.*

As he stood over the letter on the kitchen table, Doug Honeycutt marveled at the wisdom of those words, regardless of whether they made any sense, because they did and didn't, depending on the wind, and heard the truck come into the yard and his older brothers come up the steps. Like all the men of the clan they were small boned, blond, and leathery.

"Hey, seen the letter?"

"Maybe we can finally own one these things."

"Need to talk about that. The three of uth we could maybe get one farm. I'm thure McKee would cut uth a deal, and we're in pretty good thape at the bank," said Dale, the eldest brother and husband to Gladys's.

"Our wives are all for it, so what we waiting for?" said Doug.

His older brothers glared. They wouldn't bring up his separation from his wife or that other stuff, but it rankled.

"We'll have us a set-to, talk it over," added Durwood, the middle brother and Gladys's brother-in-law.

"We can't wait too long."

As the men discussed the issue, Gladys Honeycutt and her sister Betty slogged their way upslope from the lagoon decked out in their rubber boots, one-piece coveralls, hard hats and oxygen masks. Gladys, a cheery strawberry blond said:

"That drain is messed up for sure." Betty marched on, ruffling her hair.

"You know them. They're gone sink us so deep we won't never see daylight."

Gladys saw that the plan was a huge risk. But would it really change anything? That was the point she'd argued with Dale.

"I know what you mean, but look at the bright side, we—"

"Bright side! That's what Durwood ain't got, and he's fixin to have a sore head to go along with it!"

"I'm not saying it's a good idea, it's just that we could all live together, stead of you over here and us way over there: one big happy family."

They sat on the steps of Betty and Durwood's clapboard house and removed their boots and gas masks. While Betty went in for a couple of beers, Gladys frowned over the flowerbeds. Nothing would grow there, and it was the same at her own house, and everywhere around. To keep their lagoons from overflowing they followed the practice of spraying the waste on cropland, and what evaporated returned as ammonia gas that killed every garden she ever planted. It wasn't the odor, but it sure would be nice to have some daffodils. Betty returned with two cans of Schlitz, and they chatted and drank as the setting sun washed a rusty pall over the panoramic lagoons, casting in their fetid ambrosia the glow of languid ponds.

2

Randal and Elmer parked their bikes in the yard and sat back on the porch steps with beers.

"I figured you were smart, yessiree, but never would a guessed a financial genius," said Elmer. They'd been discussing the sale of the blade for several days; Elmer couldn't get it out of his mind how his buddy had so outfoxed him.

"Of course, I'm not mad or anything. Shoot, I came out pretty good, didn't I?"

"We both cleaned up, that's the way I see it. I got a load of cash and a great bike," said Randal, "and you also got some cash and that car fixed," indicating the Rambler station wagon nestled in weeds, its nose poked from an outbuilding.

"Damn sure did," said Elmer, who mashed the empty can and went inside for another as he thought: there's a real change come over that boy; he's a different person.

Sipping his beer, Randal felt like he could reach up and touch the treetops. He knew he was ready. For what, he wasn't sure, but a hundred thousand told him he was in control. Be it the road or just kicking back, when it came time to jump, he would jump. Elmer returned at sat down beside him.

"Hey now, how come what I wrote up for you and this newspaper article aren't the same?" asked Elmer, holding them side by side. "I like mine better, "The Battle of Chickamauga Twice." He began reading aloud as Randal remembered his last interview and how disappointed he'd been when Mr. Ramseur had pared away most of it. It might have had my name on it, but it sure wasn't me. But he was getting used to it, and to the byline, and he hadn't ceased to thrill at the power of addressing himself with the tag, *of the Raleigh News.* It was four articles now, and as long as played the part of a college student, he'd be okay, lies notwithstanding.

"Elmer, you can still get famous. I'm going to write about you and your store. So, I need a lot of details about rifles and ammo and stuff, and then we need to sit down with that digital recorder and you just talk away. How's that sound?"

Elmer imagined that this could lead to bigger things, maybe even his own newspaper column. He could lease the store to his uncle Rudy who wanted it anyway and had proven his mettle by trying to burn it down twice already for the insurance money, or so he'd confessed from jail.

"See, it's got to have a southern theme, so this will work out well," said Randal. He felt again the power surge of being in charge, and it felt good; it felt really good. Things had begun to turn around for him since he'd moved; the main thing, he had become a confidant of L.D. McKee who was more like a father to him than his dad had ever been. When he left, he'd cleaned out the attic of everything that was in any way connected to General Poe, and he was gradually feeding it to his mentor. In return, L.D. had been teaching him the practical merits of capitalism; buy cheap and sell dear. With his mentor's backing, Randal had acquired a BBQ stand and stock in a trucking company, Southern Pride Freight Lines. He thrilled to discover that there were ways to make money without working. Mostly, he sat in the back bedroom that had formerly housed Buster Butkins and played with stock options on his laptop. He'd been lucky so far, and L.D. had told him to run with it as long as he had it. Now, as Elmer began again to read aloud, he reviewed his plan. The BBQ joint would just be takeout, although a picnic table or two outside wouldn't hurt. He pictured starting a chain and making TV commercials. What's cool, he reasoned as Elmer droned on, is that he even had time to ride his bike and do re-enactor stuff while writing his column for the newspaper. Recently he'd picked up some pointers on journalistic style and also on college lingo so that he could continue to impress Mr. Ramseur. It happened when Eddie Terrell had stayed at Elmer's place following the re-enactment of the battle of Jezebel Tavern. Eddie had a friend along and the four of them had gotten drunk the night after the battle, with Eddie and Elmer making up for the past. They'd enticed the employees of an escort service to stay long into the night and sprawled naked on the porch in the crisp fall air, slobbering like babes and babies.

The new guy, about Elmer's age, was named Coleman Sweenie and he hailed from the Blue Ridge. Randal surmised that this was the true mountain man look: tall as a pine but clear cut above the ridgeline of eyebrows, and he read *life experience* in Sweenie's baby blues that also showed a keen interest in Randal's journalistic exploits.

"I can help you edit these reports. I've been to college," said Sweenie.

"Where'd you go to school?" Randal heard his voice from far off as though spoken from inside a tube at the other end of which his hangover received the echolalic message.

"Out west, it's kind of a long story."

"Tell it like it is, brother," said Eddie, stirring Jack Daniels into his coffee.

"It was in San Francisco after I got out of the army and got divorced too."

"Now there's a double whammy," noted Elmer.

"I wouldn't work a straight job. You lose all your money to the government. What's left won't sustain a mouse."

"What'd you eat?" asked Elmer as he sunk into a honey bun.

"I panhandled," and he went on to relate his tale. "I became a professional beggar… met this guy who told me two things. First, I was on his turf and I'd have to move on. When I pointed out that I wasn't bothering anyone, he told me I could take classes on begging strategy and tactics, and that a diploma would get me authorized for a specific piece of ground, although I might have to co-op for a while with another grad. Space was tight just then. Well, I asked him how I was supposed to pay for classes when I didn't even have enough to eat. They had that sewed up, too. At St. Anthony's soup kitchen, they always needed a pot walloper. You worked off your tuition. They supplied a laptop for taking notes and storing lessons. I learned a lot. That's where I also met some famous tax resistors and soldiers of fortune."

"So, you say it's more to it than just asking for change?" said Eddie.

"My goodness, yes! Each begging strategy had an alternate plan," he explained. "Why, you couldn't just shove your hand in someone's personal space. This was California! You had to finesse the pitch and the tone too had to be just right, the texture, the whole damned enchilada." Randal pictured a road map California as a massively tumid enchilada as Sweenie stated that the key was the mark. Once you learned how to spot the pushover, it was simply a matter of cut and run.

"Separate 'em from the crowd like a cutting horse to a steer and run your story," he said. "We had live rehearsals: the student wore a microphone and transistor, with the teacher sprawled in a doorway wearing a Walkman. I have to tell you, the written tests were a piece of cake, after all, it was only structure and methodology, but those live exams were ball busters. There was many a would-be bum that got put on a bus by PIC and sent on down the road. It was a shame in a way. After investing all that time and trouble, the last thing they'd hear would be their rejection: "Don't come back, pal, you'll never make it in this town."

"What's PIC?"

"It's the Pan-handling Institute of California, although it used to be PINC when they had to separate the northern branch from the one in Orange County, but that one went down in a corporate takeover by DEALA."

"I've heard of them," said Eddie. "It's Dealers Educational Authority, Los Angeles. They don't take just any crack dealer, you got to be dedicated and have a proven track record of vicious behavior."

"So how long were you there in Frisco?" said Randal, with the thought that he too was panhandling, but outside journalism's backdoor.

"Six years, and I made good money: enough to put me through tax resistors school from which I transferred to Minute Man Community College for Journalism."

Randal was bowled over, and accepted Sweenie's offer to edit the newspaper articles, reasoning that Mr. Ramseur would be less likely to check up on him if the articles were well crafted.

"Randal, you can do something for me too."

"Will if I can."

"I run a militia and we need financial assistance." Randal asked him for a figure.

"Well, I haven't got the books with me, but I can give you ball park."

"Batter up," contributed Elmer, as Sweenie gave a quote.

"I'll lend it to you against your editorial fee," said businessman Randal. "I'll fax you the pieces and you can fax them back."

"Just the fax, ma'am," said Elmer. Eddie's guffaw sprayed a mouthful of coffee and Elmer grabbed him by the throat and they circled, inches apart.

"Captain," said Sweenie.

"Captain?" said Randal.

"Sir!" snapped Eddie as he left the room. Soon, the militiamen were gone.

~ ~ ~

Downtown, Dr. Titus Shell admired the display in the museum's Civil War gallery. The brass plate would identify the item and name its contributor, Mr. Randal Poe. Shell walked around it again, pausing at various angles; the craftsmanship of the display would be as important as the artifact, and in this case perhaps more important, and he thought it looked good enough, and the more he thought the better it got until he saw the sword as leading the charge to gallery additions and with a new day dawning, he imagined that one day General Poe and his dog soldiers would outshine the Stone Mountain edifice in Georgia. He strolled from the gallery rubbing his hands and sat quietly in his office to await the arrival of Miller Time when he could then leave the building carrying the cursed sabre and get clean away; it might save his job if nobody looked too closely. More importantly though was the nagging, gnawing question regarding L.D. and his having gained the upper hand, once again. His attempts to contact him had been all but ulcerous until he received a welcome and an invitation to visit. Only then had he made it known at the museum that their most recent purchase was to have its provenance authenticated off-site, though he had wondered if he was overdoing it, as too many fabricated details could raise questions he wasn't prepared to answer, much less to dodge. No, he was certain that he'd done the right thing. He couldn't have met the cost of replication solely on his own, and the quoted price was only an estimate, so the only recourse, even though it turned his stomach to but imagine it, was to beg.

3

Across town Everett and Matilda sat together in front of the TV.

"First, he buys that damned motorcycle: that should have told me something." He wagged his head. Matilda picked up the remote and clicked off the set. Poe turned to her with his *how dare you* look that she'd once found so irresistible. He turned the TV back on. She assumed he'd gotten the motorcycle for Randal and hadn't given it another thought, but now realized how out of character that would be. She clicked off the TV.

"Ev, he's been saving his money ever since daddy gave him those silver dollars."

"There's more to it than that, much more."

"Well, I imagine he's feeling the winds of change like what's his name, Chance and Ariel's boy, off to Hawaii on their Beneteau—"

"There's something murky about this you're not telling me!" he snapped.

"Ev—"

"By God, woman, if you gave him money, I'll—"

"You'll what? If you knew him, he is your son after all—"

"So, it's my fault, is it? You're the one treats him like he's still in diapers for Chrise sake," and he turned the TV back on. Matilda grabbed the remote and threw it across the room.

"*I* talk to him when *I'm* not needed at the club or Rose Society luncheons and so forth. You don't realize how important that is," she said, trying to keep the edge out of her voice.

"He's got nothing to say to me that I want to hear!"

"Well, that's my point, isn't it? You've made yourself invisible."

Poe thrust off the couch. "I'll tell you who's invisible! That punk upstairs, his motorcycle and his other trash are banned from this house!" and he stormed out, leaving her shaken.

After a moment, she crossed the room, picked up the remote and returned to the couch, feeling the tension settle when she found the Home Shopping Network, her drink on the end table.

They managed to avoid each other the rest of the day in the way couples often do and Matilda soon forgot the episode, just another trivial spat. That evening in the kitchen her mind was on dinner

Everett paced as Matilda garnished a fowl.

"First, after rewriting the major scenes the Academy requested the new play and we put that together. Now they don't want it, saying they've reshuffled the play list. I said, 'alright—'"

"Ev, do you want margarine or butter?"

He stopped and glared. "I'm expounding on great and weighty issues here, and you ask me about *butter*?"

"Well, you know what Dr. Matthews said."

"Dr. Matthews can take that butter and shove it up his ass. By the looks of him, he'd probably enjoy it."

"Don't be ridiculous, he's been our physician for more than a decade. We—"

"He's a fairy."

He was ready; she could see that much: testy, irritable, and poised, and it reminded her of a Discovery channel show on the body language of sharks. Besides, all they'd done lately was fight. She ignored him as she set the table and poured a glass of wine.

"Where's mine?"

She reminded him that they no longer had a maid and whose decision that had been but realized too late that the tactic left her vulnerable. She reached for her glass and he slammed his fist on the table.

"Godamit woman, get me my wine!"

"Are you crippled, the bottle's right there," she said, pointing with her chin. He slopped wine into his glass, splashing it on her. "Pig!" He poured the remaining wine down her blouse and she shot to her feet.

"Stupid little man!"

"The pig here is you; it was *you* gave me that ingrate of a son!"

"He's not even here anymore! You ran him off!" she yelled, unbuttoning her blouse as she strode from the table. He shot past her and blocked the door.

"You're not going anywhere," he growled.

Shaking her head, she sighed and returned to the table, but when she reached for a dinner roll, he threw the basket into the air.

"You're a boy with a little dick and little sense," she laughed.

"You slut! You'd fuck up a wet dream!"

"I fucked you, didn't I?"

With a roar he raked the turkey off the table, and for a moment the baked bird flew past her glare.

"I checked the bank account because I knew you lied to me about giving him money!"

"I never gave him—"

"Bullshit," his face pushed into hers, "you gave that cretin twenty thousand dollars! Who are you, my personal fucking banker?" She rose with a punch that rocked him backward.

"The twenty gets us gilded nameplates on our putting green at the club, you gutless worm," she hissed.

"Yeah? Well, here's another payment!" he hollered, stripping off his belt as she lunged with the carving knife and then ran upstairs. After locking the door, she took a shower and a valium and then reviewed her options. These things just didn't happen in the best families! Not to the country club set. Not *us*. But lightning bolts still flashed behind her eyes, sparking deeper fires as a flickering spirit wove a garland around the spike in her heart.

4

"Hand me another sandwich, would you, L.D?" They sat on one side of the kitchen counter and drank Heineken, as L.D.'s wife made lunch on the other.

"You never could turn down a BLT," said his half-brother.

"I well remember that. Couldn't be barbeque like anybody else," she teased. "Every time you're here we make sure we got the fixings."

"Speaking of fixings," said Shell, eyeing his half-brother over the beer bottle, "there's something that needs fixing and you're the only one I trust to keep us both from going down with the ship!"

"Well, we can leave the sandwiches be for a minute. Come on back to my office and we can talk. As they made their way to the den, Shell launched his edited version of how he came to own a magnificent artifact through the reenactor association, but in spinning his yarn and drawing it out his desperation told him he was stalling.

"Have a seat Ty and tell me what's on your mind, or what's in that golf bag, one."

"What I have brought today is at the crux of this affair, and I'd just as soon get it over with than labor over the—"

"Hold on a sec. What's this about a sinking ship?" Shell told him about the museum's purchase and how an assistant had been duped but that it was *his* head on the block and that the cost of getting a replica made was prohibitive, unless maybe you're a wealthy farmer, he whined, and then that brazing company would back you all the way. Having run up the curtain, Shell extracted the blade from the golf bag and held it out in both hands as though he was surrendering, which he was, and on which he choked. L.D. saw right away the gilt initials on the hilt, but otherwise a sword like many in his collection, but he let Titus soak in his misery for a minute or two before brandishing the real McCoy and rubbing Ty's nose in it, just for fun.

"How in the hell—this is the sword *I* bought but *you* end up with it!" Contrition was replaced by an urge to wield it, but it passed just as quickly, and Titus dropped into a chair with a sigh but then shot back up.

"I'm asking you then because I just don't have that kind of, I mean our credit is good but that much I can't hide, the replication costs are outrageous, such exorbitance!"

"But when your neck is in the noose—"

"Not that it isn't worth it, but the cost—"

"Twisting on a gibbet, each quiver tightening the knot—"

"This is out of pocket, mind you—"

"Relieved at last by the drawing and quartering—"

"You're thoroughly enjoying this, aren't you?"

"Curator's torso becomes museum piece, ha-ha. Well, you have to admit to the comedy in it, Titus. Let's face it, young Poe is slicker than two eels fucking in a bucket of snot."

"The bastard! I'm hung there too; any attempt to make it a legal affair implicates me in fraudulent—"

"Hang on a second brother. Call them and stop the order on your replica." L.D. left the room while Shell made the call, aware that he'd hedged on pleading and that his half-brother still had him whole-heartedly by the testes. L.D. returned with two cold beers.

"You want to know something L.D., I don't even resent your humor at a time like this, but you ought to know what I do resent."

"Tell me, Ty." Shell spluttered and thought fleetingly of the sword and his mission.

"Mom didn't have the sense to live two states away, less two blocks; I wouldn't have known you *at all*, no football, no proms, no high school, none of that *little half* nickname crap."

"Yes, well, daddy's good business sense ran out on him the day both his partners did, I mean, who would a thunk it? But you listen up, Ty. There's been a serious wrong committed here and I aim to straighten it out, in fact, I am going to offer you a wonderful deal that will help the both of us. You're going to give me this sword you brought, but you keep the golf bag, personally I think that Spaulding has lost their spin. Here's the lay of the land: the ancestor owned two blades, this one for battle, the other for promenade, both of which I now possess in addition to a mock-up of the latter which I will lend you on a long-term lease for your display—may I suggest muted lighting and velvet ropes at a healthy remove—at a very reasonable fee."

Shell sat back down visibly relieved. "Just tell me, L.D., why you need a replica when you've got the real thing, the one that's supposed to be with *me* in Raleigh."

"Oh, you know, to play with really, I mean my own hair oil would tarnish the other inside a month. But you do that in the antiquities line as a matter of course, and you never, ever, bid on, much less accept, an item unseen; you ought to shit-can that employee if you haven't already. Now Ty, Poe pulled a fast one on you, but all is not lost."

Shell withdrew from his fugue: he figured his own deceit was justified but he'd been double-crossed and made a fool and he was determined to have a chat with Sergeant Butkins the following day.

~ ~ ~

In his bedroom at Elmer's house, Randal picked up the phone and chatted for a while with his new editor.

"Listen up, you want a hot idea, I got one," said Sweenie.

"Let her rip."

"We do a series of articles on hogs. It's the life-blood of the south, next to tobacco."

"Well, I don't know if that will wash with Mr. Ramseur. It's not exactly historical."

"Not historical? Why, a piglet marked off the Mason-Dixon Line on account they can walk a straighter line than a man; every schoolchild knows that tale."

Randal sensed that Sweenie was a step ahead.

"My sister and her family run a hog farm, and see, there'd be a topical interest aspect too. Environ-mentalists want to shut down the industry, put good people out of work. So, we turn up the heat on the human-interest angle."

"Well, as long as it sells. Let's give it a shot," replied Randal, as he leaned back in the leather chair and felt again the voltage of decision-making course through him. Outside, the cedars in the yard bent in a gust, and he moved a hand the way he imagined God would and thought about his once-devout mother who'd gone from pious when he was little to pie-eyed now, and his father lapsed and loose on his hinges. The cedars bent in another gust and he sensed that was religion enough.

"What you do is go see Gladys and them. She'll put you up. Get the lay of the land, what it's really like and so forth. Talk to my brother-in-law and also to his brothers. Carry your digital recorder."

"Also, you want to write some while you're there."

"Like first impressions."

"You got it, and when you leave you could drop the copy off up here and visit our compound at the same time," said Sweenie.

"Well, maybe. But it's getting kind of cold for the bike," he said, again noting the gray clouds skating above the cedars.

"Why not get Elmer to drive up; that old boy needs a holiday something fierce."

5

Bucolic was Randal's new word and it rolled off his tongue like a mantra as he stood on a rise overlooking an undulating landscape: a sea of pigs that stretched to the tree line. As he savored the syllables, he wrote some descriptive notes on the locale and its sharp olfactory odor before proceeding through the gates of Hogville.

In the company office he met Sweenie's sister Gladys who had been expecting him, she said, and also how nice it was that a newspaper had sent him to their assistance and was he ready to take the tour. It surprised him when she led him to a row of showers in a back hall and indicated a clothing rack in the corner. After showering, he found that the mostly one-piece mechanic outfits like Elmer wore were too big but managed to find a pair of pants he could cinch with his fingers in the belt loops. The shirt cuffs hung down below his wrists, and in the rubber boots he had to walk splay footed to keep them from sliding off. He grabbed a Redman cap and turned the bill around to the back the way he liked.

"Ready?" asked Gladys, as she poked her head around the door.

"You got to be sanitized to go inside: there's itty-bitty specks a dirt that will treat a pig mean—if you spread a germ, it could wipe out the whole farm."

"Like with the Indians," said Randal, recalling a character in one of his father's plays whose disease-infected blankets destroy a village.

"I don't know about no Indians, honey. You just come with me," and he flopped along behind her, sleeves trailing like streamers. She found a piece of wire for him to use as a belt, and they entered a barn and trudged on through a series of gates while Randal was stunned by the heavy, porcine aroma: it smells like dung in here! They exited one metal barn and entered another and he saw row upon row of stalls, and in each a dozen hogs. Or were they pigs? Some were big and some were huge, and while most were gray, others were pink. As he took it in, he listened to a choral snuffling like hundreds of people snoring, and in a flash, he knew why they called a Harley a hog. They stopped in front of a pen.

"This here's Lulu and Popsy," smiled Gladys.

"They got names!"

"I know ever one of my babies."

"You see over there," she pointed, "that's Big Mama. She's chasin' Little Mama."

Randal could not believe it. They all looked the same to him: great grunting blobs of blubber in a big box of shit. He began to feel sick.

"C'mon, I'll show you are prized possession." At the end of the row in a larger stall was the biggest hog

Randal had yet seen. It's the size of one of those, what do they call them, Chitlin Ponies. He gaped.

"This here's Uncle Ben, but I call him Doodlebug," she sang in a kewpie lilt, as the giant hog shuffled over to the fence. She scratched its head.

"You can pet him if you want." As Randal reached in, the hog snorted and with jowls aquiver clamped on the flopping sleeve, pulling Randal over the railing and into the mud. He screamed as the monster hog towered over him.

"Naughty, naughty boy! What am I going to do with you?" Gladys scolded.

"What did I do!"

"Not you, I'm talking to Doodlebug," and shook her finger. His boots had come off, and as he slithered and slipped trying to retrieve them the saucy dun-colored muck squeezed up between his toes and he spewed his ham and egg breakfast. As Gladys helped him back through the gate, he turned and saw the hog slurping his uke and he tossed it again.

"We better get you cleaned up," she said, nudging him toward a door.

Later, once showered and combed and back in his own clothes, he nursed a 7-Up as Gladys talked about the hog industry. Each confinement barn held seven hundred and fifty to one thousand head. Machines did most of the watering and feeding, and they also flushed the tons of waste down to the earthen pits called lagoons, where it was then pumped out and sprayed onto the surrounding land. She paused.

"Well, ah didn't get to introduce you to Tinkerbell: that's Doodlebug's main squeeze, and she's the pride of Bessboro."

"Why is that?"

"She's the great, great granddaughter of Bess, the founding mother, the one who started it all," she said, and left the room, returning a moment later with a framed oil painting. It depicted a hog wearing a burgundy cloak and a bejeweled crown.

"So, where is she today?"

"Honey, Bess has been dead for a hundred years."

"No, Tinkerbell."

"Oh. Well, last night she come down with a cold, so Dale, he moved her into isolation." Randal pictured the hog lying in bed with the covers up to its chin, its head adorned with a hot water bottle, thermometer in its snout.

"I'd forgot all about it when we was inside. Listen, how long you here for because what with schedules and all, Dale's the one you should talk to for facts. He knows it all."

"Remind me who Dale is."

"He's my husband, pretty much runs everything around here. You can call him Cobb, everybody does."

"Why is that, if you don't mind my asking?"

"How many ears of corn can you eat in a minute?" The question threw Randal.

"Well, he's the County champion ten State Fairs in a row. Even money says this year, too."

She shut the connecting door, and Randal worked the 7-Up and thought of pigs living like pigs and how it didn't seem right, even if they were pigs. What if they're conscious of their lodging… we assume lower mammals are not self-aware but how could you not know you lived in a box of shit; the laugh that erupted with the parallel thought of home in Umstead Mills sounded more like a hiccup and he drowned it with the last of the soda before calling Sweenie to report his experience, talk about the farm, and to ask for suggestions. He wasn't sure how to begin the article, and thought he either had too much information, or not enough.

"Fax what you've got, and I'll set it up for you," said Sweenie, who later admired his handiwork, and it occurred to him that there was more to this than bacon on the hoof: the hog farm issue was a cause célèbre and his group could benefit from free publicity, and he felt certain that they would stand out at least as much as Gladys and her tribe, known county-wide as Hogville. He too wanted a short moniker, what they had was way too long. They needed something brief and catchy like The Minutemen, but another group already had that one; all the symbolic names were taken. He didn't like it but hadn't found a way out and had to compromise and just go with the one his ex-wife had suggested, *Tax Resisters And Southern Heroes.* He picked up the framed photo of his ex and thought once again, what an exceptionally beautiful pain in the ass.

While he held the photo and traveled back to what if, at Hogville the Honeycutts sat around the kitchen table, wondering what the future might hold as the lawyer they'd hired watered down the mumbo-jumbo and went through it all again. When he left, Betty got everyone a beer.

"Two's better than one," said Gladys, breaking the silence.

"Three's better an two."

"One's better than none," said another.

"One?" they chimed.

"I thought we said get as much as we could?"

"What I say is that we don't go so far in the hole for just one farm, and look, fifty thousand head be easier to manage, *and* we manage it ourselves."

"The more stock we got the faster we pay the bank."

"I sure wish ole Doodlebug could talk," dreamed Gladys, "he'd know what to do."

"Shoot, sis, if that could talk, he'd be in here and we'd be out there!" That broke them up and they shot the breeze and guzzled suds before deciding on their best shot at Honeycutt Farms would be to contract two and let the third go. There would not be as many management problems, but they'd still have their hands full of enough mewling pork to feed every man, woman and child in a city the size of Raleigh.

8

Everett Poe sat in a booth in his favorite barbecue restaurant. In front of him were two sandwiches with slaw and hot sauce as he drank a Budweiser, and then another. He really felt more like drinking than eating, but had a hard time resisting the aroma of smoked pork. The owner, an old elbow-knocking buddy, set another cold one in front of him and said:

"I see you're in the news again."

"How's that?"

"Well, your donation to that museum."

Everett had to clear his mouth and wash it down before he could reply.

"Pearly, I don't know what you're talking about."

"Here," he said, retrieving the newspaper from the counter. Poe had been a customer for twenty years and Pearly thought he knew him pretty well, but what happened next nearly knocked him off his feet. With a howl Poe boiled up like a geyser.

"I'll kill him!"

"I'll kill him! I'll twist his neck!"

Pearly backed away in alarm, casting a glance at his customers as Poe crushed the beer cans in his fists and wheeling blindly hurled the foaming cans into the faces of two Sheriff's Deputies who up to that point had been enjoying their meal. Before Poe could put the brakes on his bubbling rage, he'd been handcuffed and duck-walked to a county car.

Pearly picked up the newspaper and looked again at the picture of a sword in a big glass box. The article said that it had once belonged to a General Poe, that it was fabled, and that the heir of Raleigh resident and noted playwright Everett Poe had sold it to the museum and it was the centerpiece of a new display recently opened to the public. As he directed the cleanup, he pondered the newspaper article and of getting on over there: whatever set off Everett like that gotta be worth seeing. And across town the author of the article also pondered.

Tarleton Ramseur sat and drummed his fingers on the chair arms. He hadn't heard from the Poe boy in some time, and he'd told Randal to check in periodically. Based on the strength of the kid's writing, he believed he had a natural, a born-to journalist, and he wanted to milk that a little further; send the boy out to do interviews. And now there had been this gap. After some checking around through his old boy network, a sketch began to emerge, one that had the earmarks of a story that all was not as it should be at the Poe palace in Umstead Mills. Mrs. Poe appeared as a besotted socialite, and her husband a firebrand with a hair-trigger temper, one who had entered academia through the back door based on the strength of his well-known play. Ramseur thumbed through his Rolodex, scowled, and punched the speakerphone.

"Archives."

"Bobby, Tarleton."

"Third time today, and this is the place for records. What's up, bubba?"

"Get me all we have on Everett Poe," and he spelled it.

"How's things up there in the daylight?" asked Bobby.

"We have this thing called a sun. I'll tell you about over a beer or three."

"You're a gentleman and a squalor, and speaking of Poe, get a load of this." And Ramseur turned crimson before he called in another favor to get the lowdown. He then left his office and drove downtown. At the Museum of History, he viewed the display, and then met with Titus Shell.

"Why, sir, I have been threatened! That man is a, a dynamo of evil! He, he, he—"

"Please calm yourself. Go splash some water on your face, I will wait." Soon enough, Ramseur learned that Everett Poe had come barreling into the museum, made a scene in the Civil War Gallery, and pursued by museum staff, he had stormed into the offices like a berserk munchkin.

"The blade is mine damnit, and I want it back!"

Determined to maintain a professional demeanor, Shell assured the guards that everything was under control, and demonstrated it by getting Poe into a chair.

"Now, sir, if you'll tell me what this is about?"

After a spluttering start, Poe wiped away spittle and told his tale.

"But, sir, the fellow, you say your son, gave me his identification and, here, let me show you." He retrieved the file believing that its contents would surely placate the man. Instead, subsequent to Poe's apoplectic reading of the bill of sale with his signature attached, assigning the bearer, Randal Craig Poe, the rights to do (with the cutlass) as he pleased, Poe howled: 'The art of our necessities is strange, that can make vile things precious,' and launched from the chair with a roar and landed on

Shell's desk, snarling, but was grabbed by the guards and hustled from the building.

Shell thanked the journalist for his visit. Just talking about it had helped to ease him, and as he put it aside, his secretary announced another visitor.

Shell smiled.

"Yes, sir, welcome to the North Carolina Museum of History, and how may I help you?" They bumped fists.

"It's a pleasure, sir, I've heard rather a lot about you."

"And I, you" They exchanged winks.

"You must mean my *collection*," said McKee.

"It may be the largest private collection of Civil War and antebellum artifacts in the state, but mine is *official*."

"Oh, come on, cut the crap, Ty, you don't own a single piece in all of it, no doubt you would; your passion exceeds mine"

"As officially sanctioned passion, technically I own it all. So, you've come to inspect our new exhibit, Leutius?"

"Well, naturally, but also, perhaps, because I already own the better half of Shives Poe."

"You can never resist a dig, can you, always reminding me of who got the better deal and why. You'll never admit that if mom hadn't jumped ship, we'd be full brothers. Instead, this better half business rings like your calling card."

"Ty, I am truly sorry if I've said something that upset you, but as one professional to another I'd like to know if I might view the Poe display, see how it looks; I may be able to offer up some advice on how not to reveal too much, but the gallery was closed."

"I don't believe a personal tour is on the menu."

"I'm just one expert running interference for all the others you'll get trooping in, I assure you, I'd hate to see things go awry."

Shell paused for a moment, looking at his folded hands so as to appear to be considering the request before denying it. He let L.D. study the brochure on his way out.

"Buy a ticket and stand in line like everybody else, *brother*."

~ ~ ~

Randal too thought of tickets: selling them. In spite of having been corralled by a giant pig, he found himself at ease in the environs of Bessboro. And like Gladys had said, the odor (that admixture so much akin to a spillage of piss, beer, and bleach) just grew on you after a while. This place is so off the wall it is way cool, he reflected, as he stood in front of the motel, freshly returned from a trip to the mountains in Elmer's old station wagon where he hadn't located Sweenie's compound but had gotten back in time to see the sign that he had ordered being hoisted from a boom truck. The Sooweet Dreams Motel and Lounge was sure to attract a livelier crowd than the old place had, so the old sign came down as new luster went on in a deal he'd struck with Cobb, who Randal now noted had a goiter on his neck the size of a hard-boiled egg.

"Gettin' too ole fer thith thit," said Cobb, a jelly glass of Scuppernong held in front of him as though he was offering it to Randal, who, mesmerized by Cobb's missing teeth, imagined the dark spaces as the sharp keys on a weathered piano.

"You lookin' at ma knob, boy?"

"No sir!"

"Hell you want."

"Think that thumthin, take a look at thith," he said, unbuttoning. Backing away, Randal said, "Uh, Cobb, sir, let's talk about making money." And that they did, once the farmer drank down to his denture soaking at the bottom of the jelly glass. As the teeth went in, the hick went out, and Randal thought that the Dale/Cobb locution must be an act.

The motel had fallen on hard times and the rooms needed repair, what with their drooping ceilings and water-stained walls of cheap veneer paneling puffed and moisture warped, mirrors chafed and cracked, and each TV was a well-abused black and white model stuccoed with cigarette burns and craters, but it beat the Poe attic as alternative quarters.

After the Honeycutt's Great Dane had peed on him, Randal had moved in. and while the air in his room smelled of wet cardboard and toe jam, it was marginally better than that outside, but he had his eye on capital improvements. "Paint's what you need," said Randal, "and some stuff to shine up that furniture, make it look new." Cobb said he'd round up some cousins could paint, and they talked up the new luster as they spent hours with brush and roller, and not only at the motel. Across the parking lot stood a defunct firework stand. When Randal was finished, it had been reincarnated as the Pig Parlor: BBQ, Hot Dogs, Burgers, and Fries. Bessboro was on the verge of entering the high stakes and exciting world of fast food. This place is going to jump, thought Randal, and I'm going to jump with it! It had become his motivational mantra.

In his room he changed clothes, nose in t-shirt against the fumes and the dresser drawer stuck again! The rickety thing wobbled, but worse, his hands came away with the tack of ageless goo. He knew one kick would end its misery, but then restoration had its limits; he couldn't destroy, how many were there, and besides maybe this thing has a history, some value. He went in search of cleaning agents and across the road he spied a plastic pail near the maintenance shed where he dumped in a double capful of 409, a jigger of bleach and some laundry detergent. Pail in hand he stepped back out and took the measure of this 'down east' as they called it: mile upon mile of flat open land that lets the sky breathe the soil and the soil drink the sky. You could put a million of anything down here and there'd be room for a million more, and he compared that to an attic and a maniac, but again was heartened by Elmer's benevolence in having offered him Buster's room, and wondered how he was doing. Back at the room, he swabbed the dresser and scrubbed a bit but then repelled by the odor and the paint he went for a drive with the windows down and chugged along in Elmer's rustbucket that shook and rattled and wheezed with every creak, and then drove back, parked at the motel, and after throttling a dog and a soda from the Pig Parlor, returned to work, steered by a sense of duty. I must have a nose for it, he laughed; he had made it a requirement that all Pig Parlor employees wore a plastic pig-nose that strapped on with an elastic string that he'd picked up wholesale from a Novelties distributor. Any customer that bought more than three hot dogs or three hamburgers would get a free pig-nose prize! Randal wore his although Cobb on occasion would swivel it to perch above an ear opposite the goiter which, Randal thought, balanced his looks, as they served the stream of vehicles lining up at the Parlor.

"They comin' from all around," said Cobb.

For two days thereafter, Randal and Cobb and some others hired from off the farm painted walls and scrubbed each room's derelict furniture, moving up the room numbers, before they ventured to return to the starting line, the dreary café.

"You know what this place needs, entertainment, like bands and dancers," said Randal.

"Strippers," said Cobb, "let's get some in here a couple nights a week. This here old lounge needs some affection."

"I'll talk to a friend of mine. He's rich," said Randal. "Get him to invest in this place."

"When you going?"

"Monday week."

"See I can't get us some ladies," said Cobb, and he grinned in shades of amber gapped with umber.

6

Everett Poe didn't really want to drive all the way to the mountains on the off chance that Randal was up there. He fidgeted and fussed for an hour as he worked on a plan to lasso his errant son and bring him to heel. Maybe a private detective, he pondered. Have him snoop around taking glossies through fences from upturned trashcans. No, that'd be a waste of money. My money! He still slow-burned with temblors of spleen at the thought of that ingrate stealing an heirloom, and then, as if that wasn't bad enough, selling to that glorified junk shop. It was going to cost him to get it back. The sword was his direct link to ancestors who, he imagined, were turning in their graves. He believed that the Poe line was destined for greatness except for occasional aberrations like his son, well, his father too, thrown in from time to time to keep the rest of them honest. I may have to purchase an offspring if I can't straighten this one out, he calculated, as he made his preparations to leave.

He stowed the rope, shotgun, and suitcase in the trunk, and the portable bar on the back seat. A momentary inspiration sent him back inside and he climbed the three flights to the attic, stopping at each landing to catch his breath. When he opened the lid of the chest and beheld the barren cavity, he had to catch his breath again.

Standing at his bar downstairs and pouring bourbon, he sensed that he didn't give a rat's ass for what may have been in that rickety portmanteau, with the exception of the pistol, which had sent him up there in the first place. 'Hell, just the sight of that old Colts hog-leg would be enough to frighten a man, and Randal's not a man. He thinks he's tough with that motorcycle. I'll show him tough.' He downed his whiskey, got in his car, and sped away.

To pass the time he listened to a tape of old radio plays, ever on the lookout for ideas or dialogue he could use. This stuff was so obscure it would be easy to lift some without anyone blinking. Hell, I've already passed that test, haven't I? When was that? And he thought back to his second Broadway play when the director had stopped production one day to confide about a line that was just too familiar, and he remembered calming the man with the assurance that it was probably the best line in the show and therefore had a life of its own. Might need a ruse to get Randal, too, but once I get the rope on him, he's a goner.

He set the cruise control and made himself a drink. As Poe drove, he noted the patches of hardwood amid the open fields and the ubiquitous tobacco barns, some of them standing since well before the Civil War. Scenes like these were steeped in him and helped to define him. He'd grown up in the Deep South and the weather, particularly the summers, had grown him as surely as had tobacco and mourning doves and heat lightening; it helped to make him a product of his environment, and he drifted back to his boyhood when he and his buddies spent every day at the creek, building dams and killing crawdads. He found the best slingshot rocks in that creek the day they'd chased a water moccasin up into the culvert that ran under the road and dared each other to run through, and only he had done it, a feat that made him king for a season. He poured two fingers of whiskey in a salute to the past as the sun winked behind the foothills of the Blue Ridge.

The next day dawned on a hung-over Poe unable to roust himself from the cafe at the Alpine Motor Lodge in Breaking Falls, a hamlet just off the Blue Ridge Parkway in western North Carolina. As he drank a third cup of coffee, he tried to assemble through the fuzz another way to come at a disturbing question, one that he refused to address even though it clawed at him; why his wife had left. Well, he wasn't entirely sure she had gone, but her absence tugged at his heartstrings as the white blood cells of denial raced to the scene and sealed the embrasure. He waited to doctor his coffee until the waitress turned away. Damned good bourbon, he thought as he lit a cigar, sweet and mellow like a good woman.

An hour later he was again behind the wheel. Seemed like as good a chance as any that his son could be at the land. Since the bequest, they'd only been up a few times; but that Randal could find it he had no doubt, but as he drove deeper into the mountains, it didn't occur to him that his heir might have been deterred by the season; if he'd known his son at all he would have understood that the motorcycle fantasy was but a warm weather bride, for the usual Indian summer had skipped this year, and it had been nippy in September. Poe, his one-track mind in abeyance beneath the throbbing tom-tom of his skull, drove on as only the driven can.

He'd always enjoyed the mountains. The crags and hidden copse of gnarled hemlock and clinging cedar ever provided him with a thrilling sense of the sinister, a foreboding that there was something out there and, by

God, you had to be a man not to let it get you. The mountains gave, and the mountains took away. Those places he'd been to as a kid, hunting with his buds, he was sure had never been traversed by another human being. Once he had left a tin of sardines high out on a cliff, at the bottom of which thundered a roiling whitewater cascade and at a dizzying angle he'd clung to roots and placed the tin just so, to alert any other hiker that might happen by that lonely and dangerous place that they were *not* the first. Later, he lamented leaving the food when his buddies wouldn't share their grub.

~ ~ ~

Though his half (assed) brother had soothed his ego with the loan of the replicated cutlass, Shell believed in playing fair and this event of the switched swords had, as he saw it, upturned the apple cart of ethics. Arriving at the gun store he was about to step from the car when he saw L.D. leave the premises. All the better, he thought, why deal with that bumpkin at all since L.D. already had, and he considered overtaking and waving him to the shoulder, but there was a police cruiser between them. When they reached open highway, he realized that his brother hadn't flown down and was now returning home. L.D.'s Cadillac was a hundred yards ahead, so Shell settled into the spirit of the chase, shadowing his brother on a state highway. He recalled that show they watched as kids, *MacGyver*, with that guy who seemed to know how to do everything. There was always an unexpected turn of events, a twist in the plot. You knew who the hero was, but he didn't always win. It separated your interest from your expectations.

An hour later he cast his eyes instinctively at the exit marker for the junction and realized that L.D. wasn't headed home after all. What in the world? Well, I've come this far, I may as well get something for my effort.

Shell tailed his brother to a country crossroads where L.D. took a room at a motel. You could count the number of buildings on your fingers. Does he have a shack-up here? That was the only thing that made any sense. Why the trip to the gun shop, then? And what was that awful smell? He wanted to know what his brother was up to, but there was no good vantage point, so he concealed himself in a group of tourists who chatted excitedly about the great adventure before them. Emerging an hour later from the hog farm tour, bewildered and disturbed, he realized how tired he was, and the lumpy motel bed only seemed to add to his weariness as he drifted off to sleep in the aromatic embrace of fresh paint.

By the following morning he grasped that he'd learned nothing, and his abiding thought was to get away from this place; it was strangely out of step with reality, with the possible exception of the strands of Christmas lights draped all over, but then, why? Otherwise, all was porcine. Even the ice cream shop with its gaudy pink sign that announced six new flavors, including pork! He'd seen a large bowl of a woman sit down to eat the house special, the Shoat Float, and he shuddered to think of the ingredients as she sprinkled Baco-Bits over the chocolate syrup. Each table had a bottle of them, next to the Sweet-n-low and the Texas Pete. That had been the last stitch. As he drove away, Bessboro in the rear-view mirror became peripheral, diminished, and then gone altogether as though it belonged to another dimension.

From a front window in the Sooweet Dreams, L.D. watched his brother drive away, pondered the oddity of it, and then turned his attention to Cobb.

"My maintenance reports not getting back to you, sir?"

"Once a month, every month, right as rain, and let me say it now, I'd like to see you keep up that track record until the sale goes through, said L.D."

"Well sir," said Cobb, "I've been with this here McKee Farms some twenty years and things is better now than ever."

"There are changes afoot, Cobb." L.D. pulled the check from his pocket and laid it face down on the table. Cobb eyed the check, licked his lips, and sat up straight.

"Little experiment while the sale is pending, I want you to get me one hundred gallons of that pond slop, how you get it—" but he was interrupted by Randle sliding into the booth.

"Hey L.D. great to see you, listen you got a minute, I could use some advice on supply and demand." L.D. slipped the check off the table and smiled at Cobb, who didn't take the hint. Well, there would be time to deal with the shady side of Randal's business acumen; it could wait, but he admired the kid's spunk, and he got an earful.

Randal's money spent on the restoration of Bessboro had infected the locals and awakened them from the slumber that was marked by centuries of tenant farming at about the time that the Honeycutts agreed to contract terms for the two largest tracts put on the market by L.D. McKee. Honeycutt Farms, or Hogville to the affectionate, was finally to come into being and the remainder of the neighborhood had hopped on the bandwagon. Cobb's brother Durwood turned over the lease to the long-defunct Sinclair service station out at the crossroads, now slated to become the Porcine Pancake House. The entire hamlet was alive and growing with new vitality, and plans were afoot for Putt-Putt golf and a souvenir stand. Trinkets had been the devoted inspiration of the Honeycutt women following Randal's first visit. Their idea was simple; if one person could be interested in a hog farm tour, why not hundreds? All people had to do was to know about it! Bessboro's denizens went yackety-yak from shack to shack on the working assumption that when tourists emerged from the big pigpens they would eagerly stock up on caps and T-shirts, key chains, coffee mugs and beer huggers and bumper stickers (Honk if you Love Pigs). By golly, this blue-chip renaissance of pork was going to put Bessboro on the map. Almost overnight it had become a destination; what had been a wide spot in the road, a blink-and-miss-it kind of place was transformed into a bona-fide *somewhere*. For one, Gladys was stunned by it all. She just couldn't see the bottom of it as she sat with Betty on the concrete steps, their hangout spot, and drank beer after beer.

"Pigs is everything and I just never saw it," she said, bewildered in the simplicity of such a complex structure.

"They the life-blood of this country," agreed Betty. "A pig would do anything for you, and they don't want nothing for themselves."

"Bacon grows a body up strong, Daddy always said. And I suspect that's why we always had chitlins for breakfast," she added, picturing her father at the table, in bibs and a bib.

"All that stuff about corn flakes an orange juice, I bet they jest paid somebody to say that!" snapped Betty, who took a hit off her beer. "Grandma always had a jar of pickled lips on her nightstand, case she wanted a midnight snack, and she lived to be a hunnerden nine." The two women sat and drank and looked out over what would truly soon be theirs.

~ ~ ~

Poe was pleased to find a lock in place on the chain that barred entry to his land. All that I came away with from dad's fabulous fucking estate, the bastard. He drove down the rutted track, door-high weeds sounding like a carwash beneath the chassis. Well, it looks like a huge piece of nothing. If it wasn't so far out in the sticks, I'd put a mall in here, a paper mill, hell, anything would be better than this! What an eye-sore! The property ran for more than four miles along the state road and was a mile deep. It was covered with pine and hickory, maple and beech. There were towering thickets so wild and broad as to be impenetrable, save by rabbits, and also one vast sea of poison ivy. The sky was a brilliant blue in that stark clean way of higher altitudes. Swaths of cloud raced overhead, but on the ground, there was only a faint breeze. Poe zipped his down vest and hefted the shotgun. There's no need for the rope, Randal's not here. Might as well look around and make sure it hasn't become somebody's dump. As he strolled, his mind drifted to the times he'd come here as a boy with his father, lawyer and lumber baron who, on his death, owned large tracts of land throughout the southeast. Just imagine, if you'd kissed his ass, you'd be a wealthy man, living on St. Kits with a harem of women instead of tromping up here in weeds looking for that bonehead. He felt a twinge of regret over those summer jobs arranged by his father with the railroad; but it was those collegiate summers in the switching yard that sowed the seeds of his disaffection with the sire's white-collar drama, supplanted by the sweat of working with his hands on freight cars and he'd hopped that train bound for glory. A rifle shot jolted him from his reverie.

"Hold it right there." Poe was soon approached by an old man holding a deer rifle at port arms, a six-footer and thin as a stick who wore one of those one-piece hunting outfits favored by construction workers. An orange cap graced his silver locks, but his features were indistinct, as Poe was facing into the sun.

"Last claim jumper I caught run off with a load of buckshot in his ass," he wheezed, his voice high and reedy, and Poe recognized it as that of his neighbor, and thought, anywhere else that would be a welcome relief.

"You can put that bird gun down gentle," wheezed the old man.

"Mr. Terrell, I'm Everett Poe."

"The hell you are. I swore I'd shoot that pint-size son of a bitch next time I saw him, and you ain't dead."

"Mr. Terrell, I—"

"Son, you're trespassin' on Republic land, a crime punishable by ten years in the ranks or death, one." Poe now wished for his father's velvet touch, that silky glibness that had allowed him to screw clients so deftly they often thanked him. Poe edged to his left to better see his adversary.

"With all due respect, sir, I have to disagree. I believe we are standing in a meadow that is contested by both Mr. Terrell and Mr. Poe," he explained, believing himself to be safer if referred to in the third person.

Terrell moved closer. "What's that?" He set down the rifle and swabbed his face with a handkerchief.

Poe went over it again but louder this time.

"That oak over yonder marks the damn line," said Terrell.

Poe looked about him and saw only pines. "What oak?" he demanded.

Terrell turned to point, and unable to find the tree threw out his chest by arching his back and said: "You just watch where you step, Shakespeare," and walked off, whistling.

Once he'd gone, Poe realized that Terrell had been toying with him. Why, if that crusty old bean pole had a brain to match his ego-the comparison went unfinished as Poe uplifted his hip flask as two turkey buzzards wheeled; twin black specks in the deep blue. He drank again and recalled his strange relationship with the Terrell family.

The octogenarian mountain goat who'd just threatened his life was one Merle Terrell, the great, great, great, grandson of August Terrell who, like Poe's father, had acquired a great deal of land through shady means. The difference was that Terrell had done it more than two hundred years ago. What's more, several deeds had been obtained through a traveling lawyer named Andrew Jackson. For several generations the Terrells eked out a living on no less than four thousand acres, not due to a lack of skills at farming and logging, but because they were shiftless and lazy.

After the Civil War, the surviving members of the family returned to their forest home to find it ransacked. There were but two Terrells left at that time, and as they began to pick up the pieces of their shattered lives, they determined to sell land to raise cash and keep the wolf from the door, as well as the blisters from their hands. To their alarm they discovered that they retained only a fragment of the deed to their acreage. They plundered the family home more thoroughly than the Yankee soldiers had, but the search failed to turn up the document. They kept quiet about the deed, fearful that if anyone found out then sure as the sunrise some fancy talkin' lawyer man would skin them out of it. Angry and bitter, they had had to go to work like everybody else.

Poe also knew that his father had discovered the missing deed and had attempted to pry the Terrells from their claim, only to come up against a foe more tenacious and diabolical than he would have thought possible from a host of shoeless sodbusters. Poe's father had met his equal somewhere up here, perhaps this very meadow, and had fled in terror one day with his fanny peppered with rock salt, but his pride and vanity wounded to the quick. Several years later he discovered an additional fragment of the deed in Jackson's papers at the University of North Carolina. Emboldened by this knowledge, he let it be known to friends in the state legislature that the Terrells held no legal documentation of ownership, even if they somehow got their hands on the Jackson fragment. Half the residents of Appalachia claimed at one time or another that Andy Jackson had supped at their table, slept in their barn, shod his horse at their smithy, or seduced their daughter behind the mill. The stories made great yarns, of course, but a yarn does not a deposition make. Poe's perfidy was never made known to the Terrells, but they hated him just the same. The land that Everett now stood upon had been purchased and bequeathed solely because it was a finger in the eye of Merle Terrell. The Poe land had access to the state road, fresh water springs, and good, rich soil, everything lacking in his neighbor's parcel of Pee Dee County.

Everett picked up the shotgun, the steel cold in his hand, and headed back to the car. What did he mean by Republic land? That hawk-nosed old buzzard, he rumbled, now angry that he'd allowed himself to be surprised, threatened by his neighbor. What goes around comes around you bony old bastard. It was his own land they'd stood on, and Poe now realized that Terrell had the run of the place whenever he wished; free to hunt and fish and even to log! The thought stopped him. He turned and looked back stunned by the certainty that Terrell was taking advantage of him. We'll see about that, and he slammed the car door. Driving back down the mountain passes he ran through splenetic scheme after scheme until he hit I-40 and the cruise control regulated cogitation to where he saw that he was clueless on where to look for his spry.

7

Randal had spent fruitless hours trying to get in touch with L.D. and he'd called and texted and watched chat tags hang unanswered and then left a voicemail asking for outside help if his mentor was preoccupied. He really needed assistance with these business dealings and it had him worried, but not so much as to prevent the bikini-clad girl on the Harley, an amalgam of Audrey and others, from getting in the way, but why did she arrive so often when he was sweating something, when he had unanswered questions and no one to turn to?

In an odd sort of delivery, a man walked in and introduced himself as Aaron Salmon. His business card read: Sales, Distribution, Marketing: Capitol Foods, Richmond Virginia. He wore a gray three-piece suit, and Randal noted the wiry black hair was a lot like his own. Salmon's thick lenses made his eyes swim, a feature that went along with an excitable agitation: one that at first saw him sit, then stand, then pace as he explained the reason for his visit but sat back down before he had finished a completed thought or completed a finished thought. To remain top-notch competitive, he said, shuffling through his briefcase while he droned on, diversification has become the mother of invention.

"Wasn't that a band way back?" asked Randal.

"We can register Sow Syrup with a trademark and distribute this fine product for a pittance of its wholesale price. Here," and he extracted a folder from the depthless briefcase, but then he sensed a neophyte and so downshifted and carefully explained how he'd come across a bottle of the pork-chop flavored soft drink the Honeycutt's were vending, though it tasted more like licorice, and then went through the figures until Randal was shaking his hand. As he departed, he left a packet of brochures on Capitol Foods. Randal felt a huge weight removed, as though he would soar to greater heights. He was now part of a big corporate family. And Salmon too congratulated himself on another egg in the basket. They might yet heal the ailing giant. Of course, if management didn't live lean, yet there were too many variables, too many imponderables and uncharted possibilities just yet, but he was upholding his end. The company wouldn't sink on his account.

With the interview concluded, Randal had gone out to mail some letters, and on his return, he was approaching Bessboro when the car died, rolling to a rattling halt. It wouldn't start again, and he had no idea what might be wrong with its forty-five-year-old engine. Opening the creaky door and stepping from the car, he zipped his jacket, and began to hike.

Soon after, L.D. McKee's Lexus came around the curve as he headed out of town and recognizing the car, he pulled in behind it and got out. Looks like the vehicle that hick described, a rust-bucket with fins. It didn't take him long to find the title, registered to one Elmer Wayne Butkins. Beneath the odor of ammonia that hung in the air like a shroud, he thought he smelled something else. Sure enough, as he raised the hood, he knew the block was cooked and he didn't bother with burning his fingers to check the bone-dry radiator.

So, the kid was still around, somewhere. He stood beside Elmer's dead heap and reviewed what he knew so far. He'd seen his brother's car at the motel, confirmed by one Shell Smith in the guest book. Why would Ty come to a place like this? It didn't take him too long to conclude that it was for the same reason he had, and there was just one source for all that anguish over the swords, most recently the seller of an 1863 Colt revolver. All those items had once belonged to the same man.

Further, the museum had been duped in the sale. If you put it all together, the kid was one sly operator. Ordinarily, he wouldn't care, as he was no stranger to shady deals, after all, it was underhanded transactions that livened up a staid business world, but the kid had burned his brother; there will be some recompense. I think I know just what to do, and he plotted his moves as he headed back to Bessboro where in the newest double-wide a party was in progress.

The Honeycutts were now the sole contractors of what would become Honeycutt Farms, their very own.

"Someday all them little Hogville darlins will be ours," rejoiced Gladys.

"We'll be able to fix up the place," chimed one.

"And real nice clothes for the kids!" added another.

"New cars too!"

"Hang on y'all, just hang on," said Dale. "We got to pay the bank first, that's the main thing, but first we got to make us okay."

"Aw Dale, don't spoil the fun."

He got up and left, passing Randal on his way in. A glassy-eyed Gladys pulled Randal aside, hauled up to his ear and whispered, "Doug's lookin' for you but don't pay it no mind—he lost that one."

"What? Hey, whose birthday is it?" said Randal.

"We celebratin, honey. The man finally put us in charge, and the bank give us the money."

"Hey, that's great," said Randal. "Listen, can I use the phone?" He called Elmer first and gave him the news. Elmer replied that the old girl had been living on borrowed time, and for him not to worry about it.

"Listen," Elmer continued, "next weekend I'm headin' up the mountains now me and Eddie patched things up. Why don't you come along?" After some calculations, Randal agreed.

"Look, I'm going to have a truck," said Randal, "so if you can get down here, we'll ride up together."

Randal found a can of Bud and then called Sweenie. The recording told him to hang up and try the number again and on the third attempt he remembered Eddie's card.

"Tax Resisters And Southern Heroes."

Randal looked again at the card.

"May I ask who's calling?"

"My name's Randal."

"Coleman. Up here, security is our business. Tell me, how did you get ahold of this number?" Randal explained his Chickamauga encounter.

"Ok. I got two phones up here. One's for the militia and the other for journalism and stuff. We won't have snoops. Listen, I sent everything out to that Ramseur."

"You include the pictures I took?" Randal was assured that his best yet was on its way to the Raleigh News. Later, he realized he'd forgotten to tell Sweenie that he and Elmer would be up the following weekend. Well, Elmer knew the way.

The next day Randal and Cobb hiked through the maze of hog pens and yards, skirting the berms of waste lagoons to visit a good old boy and second cousin twice removed from the Honeycutt line. Randal thought they'd never stop bumping fists. Out back of the guy's house sat an ancient Chevy panel truck, painted army drab green with worn badges of poorly sanded putty splotches on the quarter panels.

"I know it don't look like much from the outside, but check this out," and he lifted the hood to reveal a new engine that barely fit the compartment.

"Had it special fit for this here truck and she's got power to spare, I shit you not. Got a 289, and three deuces in her, and she'll flat out fly." Then they looked inside: the seats were stepped nip and tuck maroon leather and behind, the bed was a retrofitted three-quarter inch sheet of furniture-grade oak plywood that curved around the wheel wells like sexy hips. By the end of the day, it was Randal's. Way cool! He entered the motel cafe to get a Coke and was elated to see L.D. sitting there and slid into the booth.

"Hey Lou, I really got to tell you this strip—dancer dragged me into bed and man she was wild! It was great really great! We musta humped the foam right outa that bed! Her skin is like incredible! Well, I mean, I guess they all have it, right, all of 'em smooth, so cool you know, well hey you probably, is every time going to be rock-n-roll like that, you're married and all and you and your wife—"

"Randal, I'm glad as hell you lost your cherry, but we have some serious business to discuss. Take a ride with me."

"Yeah, I want your opinion about some business. I might be in over my head."

McKee smiled at the thought: You've got that right. They left the cafe in L.D.'s Lexus and drove out past the interstate where the land was flat for miles. Only Bessboro seemed to have definition in the down-east geography. Randal couldn't hear the heater like he could in his truck, but man was it warm. L.D. broke the silence of the heat.

"Where did you get that sword?" Randal told him.

"What about the one you sold the museum in Raleigh?"

"Oh, shit," he said, and hedged that it was only after selling L.D. the commemorative sword that he remembered he had a deal with Dr. Shell and had just given the curator his grandfather's other sword, the one he'd carried into battle.

Well, thought McKee as he drove, it doesn't really matter. "My brother fronted the money for the museum, so he's the one you ripped off."

"What's your aim," asked Randal, scrambling for a back-door plan. The car was an oven.

"I'm going to turn your name over to the police unless you do what I tell you." McKee felt the luxury of control wash over him, a sensation he never tired of.

Randal scoffed, why his father's law—shit, but he had capital M money, the toothpaste of judges—damn, that's gone too?

L.D. drove for a while thinking: he liked the boy, thought he saw some real spunk there, but generosity ruined the fun when you had someone twisting in the wind.

Randal ruminated while running through his available options which were too often guided by experience in familial denial, then stalled while he ticked off approaches and outcomes until he felt cornered, the privilege candle guttering. L.D. seized that crestfallen moment to pounce.

"I expect you to reimburse the money I paid for your sword, every last penny," and he turned with a grin that made Randal sick. He'd spent gobs of that money. The rest was in the bank.

"Can we make some kind of deal?"

L.D. was silent as he mulled scenario. "What did you have in mind?"

"Well for starters will you turn the heat off? I mean like, you have the sword that granddad got from General Stuart; you got that .44 pistol too."

"What of it?"

"Well, I also got his uniforms, boots, hats, gloves, cartridge belts, letters and stuff and maybe a map case."

L.D.'s eyebrows went up an inch.

"Impressive, but all of that wouldn't amount to a quarter of the value of that saber, surely you must know that." They came up behind a line of cars at a railroad crossing. The crossbars were down, and the signals were flashing; and though the horizon was clear for miles and it was obvious there was no train in that county, they sat, and for Randal that absurdity was the final straw. He then waxed about Sow Syrup and they only needed a little more capital invested before it began to pay off; if he couldn't do it now, it was going down the tubes; it was his only chance, he sang, and hoped he hadn't overworked the adjectives! McKee, inured to purblind ass kissers, half-listened to the fuzzy logic: pretty soon he'd be cleaning out the Honeycutts, and now he could sink some of that back into Bessboro? It was laughable, but why not have some more fun? From what he'd seen, the place seemed to attract suckers like a bug light. In the end, I'll get all of Shives Poe, save the corpse, and a steady flow of the wages of sin from Randal's pockets. I love it!

They returned to Bessboro and wrote out an agreement. McKee made out a check to Randal, half down and the other half upon delivery of the general's accoutrements. Randal would then have ninety days to make good on his commitment or go to jail. L.D. had no doubt that his little act of generosity would spark the boy on the road to recovery. A dejected Randal watched his livelihood drive away and didn't see Doug until he was in his face: "You stay away from her Randal! She's family, we clear on that?!"

Book Three

The Republic of PeeDee County

Tarelton Ramseur stood the brochure on his desk and pondered, looking beyond the museum's latest exhibit as sirens sang again their doleful hymns beckoning him to a time that *never was*, a la Thomas Wolfe, never again to be the same; glimpses into the past that were spared of the romantic, like a copy of a masterpiece, especially the photogravures with their haunting stares, wrapped snug in that essence of a period gone. He focused on the photo captions and puzzled over the glaring misprint. Typos were the bane of an editor's eye, and a class act like that of the museum's media office wouldn't be so sloppy, would they? He punched an extension on his speakerphone.

"Archives."

"Hey Bobby, Tarleton."

"Sup bubba?"

"Run a name for me: Titus Shell," and he spelled letter-by-letter the given name.

"You ought to have a direct line down here."

"You're it. And this one's worth a six pack."

At home that evening he explained to his wife over dinner that his query hadn't resolved curiosity as much as deepened it.

"The museum purchased the Poe sword via the philanthropy of its curator, Titus Shell."

"And that rang a bell?" asked Carolotta, a stout blond in a sundress the size of a pup tent.

"Not exactly, but it's not a common name. He turns out to be the half-brother of one of the biggest period collectors in the state, for that matter, the South," he said, pointing at the chicken platter. She passed it and then handed a succession of bowls.

"I don't see the angle, dear," she said.

"Well, why would L.D. McKee's half-brother not purchase the item for the family?"

"Perhaps they have a competition," she said, buttering a biscuit.

"That's when I really began poking around, and with the help of a few friends—"

"Six, wasn't it?" She winked.

"Why yes it was, peach fuzz, and my how it emboldens the appetite." Together they made the cobbler disappear from the tray, and a well-rehearsed dispersal cleared the table and loaded the dishwasher, the lone extravagance they'd allowed in the rustic home. Once settled in the den with a coffee she nudged him back to his tale.

"Well, I ran all the names and learned that Everett Poe was recently arrested on a drunk and disorderly. Apparently, he's quite the dynamo; it wasn't the first time he'd been taken downtown, nor was it the first time he'd blamed his behavior on his son. The upshot is that he claimed in the statement taken at the hall that the sword had been sold behind his back. However, the previous complaints against his son proved bogus."

"Well, I got the feud right, but the wrong family, I guess," said Carolotta.

"You've always had it, babe," winked her husband. "So, I visited the museum and found they have a bill of sale signed by the playwright."

"So that's it, except it is not."

"Not quite. I was disturbed by the arresting officers' remarks. They claimed that the elder Poe was threatening the life of his son, and according to the

Sheriff's department, they have been out to the Poe residence numerous times."

His wife rose from the settee and opened a cabinet and withdrew a pair of brandy snifters, motioning him to go on.

"So, my thoughts turned to Randal."

"He's such a nice young man."

"And since I hadn't heard from him in a while, I called the college."

"Well, it's a wonder they'd tell you anything. It's not like it used to be."

"No, it isn't, but I've got a few old shadows still haunting the corridors."

"Where don't you have them?" she asked, raising her glass. They drank and nuzzled and then had another one.

"Sweet, they don't have a Randal Poe. I ran it down, and the kid just isn't there. Based on what he told me, I have to assume I've been hoodwinked, but instead of ticking me off as it should, I find that I'm worried, concerned for his safety." They sat a while.

"What can we do, bubba, but save him from his father?"

"Amen, sister, amen."

"But first we'll have to find him," she said.

"My lovely peach fuzz, behind every journalist is a bloodhound. With you by my side, we'll dog his trail," and they nuzzled away.

~ ~ ~

The day had dawned warm and breezy and promised more of the same along the Blue Ridge, with the nights cool but pleasant, and Coleman Sweenie cracked the windows before opening the mail and discovering delightful news, the best he'd had in a long time. As Commandant of the militia group, Tax Resisters

And Southern Heroes, he was excited to have a great announcement to make to the troops, but tact was essential. Passing a memo down through the chain of command would be inappropriate to the occasion. Pacing in front of the windows, he paused to watch private Dewit entranced over a lawnmower, and he hit on a plan that came in a single word: Jamboree.

"Sergeant," he said into his phone. A moment later, Sergeant Lynette Stratt entered and he explained what he wanted from the troop without letting the cat out of the bag. She saluted, spun on her heel, and marched out of the office.

She was a thickset woman with crew cut red hair, formerly an animal trainer with the Ling-Puddle Family Circus, but her career as a hippodrome heavy ended when the owner, one Oliver Ling-Puddle, was caught plumbing a chimpanzee during Lent and on an Easter Sunday in Bluff, North Carolina, Sweenie had recruited her before the circus was run out of town.

The way she spit tobacco reminded Sweenie of his mother. He admired her swagger, that she was the most adroit in the subject of guns, and Sweenie's estimation of her capabilities had proven correct as she had shaped a ragged and ragtag cadre into a well-regulated militia. Why, even Dewit, who was often slower than sunbaked mud, had shown improvement.

After calling the troop to attention, she issued her orders, and the boys went to different areas of the common room to begin their tasks. Lynette sat down across from her pet peeve Private.

"Listen up," she said, "we're gonna invite all the other groups like us to a big pow-wow."

"What you said."

"And I'm saying it again. Make sure it gets through that dirt dobber's brain. I'm a dictate and you're gonna write it down," she stated, and began with the headline the Commandant had provided, but then she stopped him.

"It ain't *malisha* you dumb-ass, it's more than one," she said.

"Okay then," and he crossed it out and then wrote *malishas.*

"You can't even spell it!" she barked.

"Spell this," he said, but she stared him down.

"Alright, you're so damn smart, you spell it."

"I can spell it, you bet your ass I can spell it."

"Starts with an M."

"I know what it starts with, dickweed. It's M-A-L-I something. I about had it but lookin' at you scared it off." She got up and marched to the door of the Commandant's office, faced with a tattered America Wants You, Uncle Sam's skeletal digit extended.

"Sir. Trooper Stratt requests permission to use the dictionary."

"At ease, trooper. It's over there on the shelf." She returned to the table.

"Sure as shit, here it is. I was right, I knew I was right, it's M-A-L-I-C-I-O-U-S- Malicious."

~ ~ ~

The Raleigh News ran a featured article titled The Bessboro Renaissance that also made the Charlotte papers. It displayed photos of the new motel and some of the denizens of the *reawakened* and *quaint* hamlet, but then got its digs in about the gagging ammonia, with a reference to 'miasmal vapors' that were 'the hallmark of industrial pork.' The article suggested that visitors make the trip on a windy day. The extended family was again gathered in one of the houses where they had begun meeting regularly, now more as a company than those related by blood, although Gladys made sure to tape the newsprint story to the living room wall.

"Hey, don't get discouraged. I learned in community college that even bad advertising is worth something. Besides, they said more good things than bad," said one as they discussed the news. Doug ignored them while he inwardly smoldered over the photo of Randal wrapped around his ex and the caption about lovebirds in a parkland of pork.

"Seems like they could a said our names, instead of Randal. It ain't fair," said Betty.

"There's only one Honeycutt Farms in town, and that's us."

"Randal put us back on the map, what he did," added Gladys, "he oughta be the mayor. You look over there," and she pointed out the kitchen window to where the top half of the Ferris wheel's lights loomed against the soft glow of backlit neon.

"Before, we was just farmers, now we going to be famous. They could make a TV show about us," she dreamed aloud, still gazing out the window. Durwood had been listening to the parley, nursing his beer. He was troubled by a call he'd received offering a bid on the farm that had confused him, but he hadn't said anything about it yet, had to think on it, and now he hoped that this public attention would somehow be helpful to them all.

Among those who saw the article on Bessboro was an elated Everett Poe who corralled a posse of tools and made plans to go after his errant son, but Tarleton Ramseur had gotten the jump on him with an RFD number and a map.

The focus of many other readers, however, was concentrated on the larger issue of pollution as a threat to their livelihood. Since the Neuse River fish kills several years back had been traced to a toxic microbe in hog waste, the hue and cry had been raised. Downstream lay one of the state's greatest natural resources in the Pamlico Sound and its neighboring six others (Albemarle, Core, Croatan, Currituck, Bogue and Roanoke) that make up the second largest estuary in the United States.

~ ~ ~

"Thing ith," said Cobb, as they stood in front of the motel, "we got uth a problem, and I'm too old for them kind of hourth, but I got couthinth, nephewth, all kind a folk can help uth out."

They went inside and sat in a booth in the cafe, daylight dull in the orange plastic, and Cobb ordered coffee and a Coke and soaked his denture in the latter before inserting it in his mouth.

"What's going on?" said Randal.

"I took the cousins off the motel and put 'em on the berm. They've done good work so far, it's best to hang on to them."

"What's a berm?" Cobb leaned in and whispered, although they were the only customers.

"You keep this to yourself: we got us a leak. But they shoring it up and we'll get 'em pumping off the rest."

"You mean one of the lagoons is leaking?"

"It happens from time to time, no big deal we keep on it."

"Are you sure they can handle it?" asked Randal.

"My sister's cousin's family, you know."

"Well, if they're up to it."

"We're outgrowing at shed too. What we need, Pig Parlor and Sow Syrup too, is a barn," said Cobb, "or something like it."

Randle sensed the wonderous oddity, momentarily caught again by Cobb's wiser than he looked and dumber than he sounded bifurcation.

"How about one of those steel buildings they've got out there by the inter-state? They say you can put them up in a day." Cobb nodded and smiled, and his weathered skin wrinkled up like beef jerky.

"Sonny boy, our profits on the Syrup gonna take care of us, you wait and see," and with a wink he drank from his mug.

"You go ahead and order that shed and I'll meet you and those boys at the berm," and they left the cafe as two tractor-trailers pulled in.

The strip tease at the motel was really becoming a draw. Randal marveled how it was like a circus for the big kids as he climbed into his seat on the Ferris wheel for what would be his seventy-fifth ride. He'd seen Rose and Darlene take off their clothes so many times that he'd taken to riding the wheel between the acts, the *swoosh* of air as he was lifted up, the chair swinging with the momentum, but the best part was the view; day or night it held the eye: the rows of silver containment barns like furrows in a sheet metal garden, shimmering in the sun, and ghostly reflective in star light.

Yet on this day his mind was on the impending arrival of the bumper cars he'd ordered, his last great inspiration before L.D. had ruined everything. They were going to have pig-shaped cars, piglet coupes and compacts that you drove around and smashed into others. That's going to be way fun, he thought gleefully, the big wheel coasting to the top again where he could see over the gleaming barns to the tree line and where at a vacant tractor shed cum bottling plant his salvation churned in vats.

As Randal left the ride, Doug stood blocking the exit and the baseball bat seemed to speak his voice: "Randal, I told you once. I catch you with her again I'm give your ass its own zip code." Shouldering past him Randal thought about Missy during and after her dances and how every eye turned and how she got more whistles than a toy store and all that jealous attention surely did polish his ego, but something seemed out of whack, and had been, 'like a north and a south' said a voice.

He got into his truck, which he'd decided to name "Peaches" after his favorite fruit, and from a cooler he kept between the seats he pulled a bottle of ice-cold Sow Syrup and sat for a moment sipping, mind's eye fixed on Missy, before driving out of the parking lot past the pancake house, the souvenir store, the quick mart, and suddenly into the countryside where a hook left took the dirt road that followed the creek and ended in a stand of scraggly dust-covered pines. Nodding to the cousins who stood with Cobb, the four walked behind the flatbed truck on which stacked fifty-five-gallon drums were roped to the bed and others formed little pyramids near the tailgate. Cobb taught the boys how the hoses were attached.

"Usually helps to have one guy holding the hose on this end because it'll jump on you when you least expect it," he said.

"What about over there," said one of them, pointing.

"That's the sump pump, and it's tighter than a bearcat's bunghole, don't you worry 'bout it," said Cobb, who went on to instruct them on other details, where they kept the gasoline for the pump, spare filters and other supplies. Randal noted the location of the sump at the foot of the berm, its plastic embrasures, and the gloss of the new pump. Well, okay.

"Don't ever turn off that pump, boys. You spill gas don't worry about it; you spill seep, same thing. You gotta change barrels, just lay at hose in the creek there, that way you don't get it all over you," instructed Cobb, but to Randal there was something wrong in it, and he pondered as he and Cobb walked back to the truck.

"They'll be fine long as you pay 'em more than you was up to the motel."

"The going rate's what, maybe seven, eight an hour," said Randal, feeling his way.

"Ten," said Mr. Cobb.

"Ten bucks!"

"Listen, we pay 'em decent we get loyal workers. They be there when they supposed to; be dedicated; won't let us down; most important," and he drew Randal to the other side of the truck, "I ain't got to remind you, is they gonna keep they mouths shut," said Cobb. Randal sensed he was pushing his luck; something was awry.

~ ~ ~

The Ramseurs drove up and parked at the motel and got out and looked around. The hog farm entrance and offices were across the road, adjacent to a ticket booth and sign that read HOGVILLE TOURS, $6.00. Completing the purview was a take-out place not much bigger than a broom closet, a pancake house, and behind the motel some carnival rides that stitched locale to the horizon, green and brown hues against the pale blue Carolina sky.

"The air, it's disgusting," said Carolotta, her nose wrinkled.

"Ammonia," said Tarleton. "The people here breathe this as a matter of course."

"It's making me dizzy," she declared, leaning on the car. There was no one in sight, and Tarleton noted the absence of birdsong. Moving toward the office he heard a door shut and turned in time to see a dark haired, partly clad woman leave one of the motel rooms and enter another.

"Over there," said Tarleton, "the truck." She saw it too. An old panel truck sat nose in to the curb with a personalized license plate that read: CUTLAS. The woman who'd appeared a moment before emerged again, dressed in a uniform.

"Y'all need a room?" she asked.

"No, thank you, miss, we're here looking for Randal Poe, his parents are worried about him," said Tarleton, off the cuff. The waitress' nametag identified her as Missy, and she took both of Carolotta's hands in hers and said: "Your son is a fine young man, you should be very proud of what he's done for all us here," and as she entered the cafe she said, "number six."

Randal thought he was dreaming. Missy Rose had been rolling in his arms, and then the next thing he noticed was her sitting at the foot of the bed, rolling hose up her legs, sex delirium again, an elixir, an exotic drug that expanded his mind and shot his body into the heavens before it gentled him back to earth like a feather, like a stone to its river bed, and he had never slept so well before that he could remember. Now, coming out of another dozing, Missy Rose had become Mrs. Ramseur: surely a trick of the drug; he kicked at her and said: C'mon sweet thing, don't leave now, let's go again, but before he got the words out, a chuckling fat lady had grabbed his ankles and raked him from the bed.

"M-M-Mizz'z Ramseur!" he cried from the floor. Shaking the cobwebs from his dream head. Tarleton loomed.

"Randal, we need to talk. We are quite concerned about you, and we don't want to see you hurt. Please get dressed. We'll be outside, okay?"

Randal stood in the lot staring after the car as it drove away. 'Damn! That's got to be a classic double whammy, as in the books. Well, I don't need the newspaper column; this is where the money is. Besides, I can freelance now anyway, enough people will have seen my name.' But he felt bad for deceiving the Ramseurs earlier, and again just then. They'd offered to put him up, his own room, until he worked things out with his father, and he'd gone along with it, his head bobbing on a spring as he agreed to their suggestions, grateful for another chance, but only after he'd cleared up some stuff, about which he'd been vague. They had hugged like Russians with Mr. Ramseur assuring him everything would work out. He saw Cobb taking the sun on the motel steps and joined him.

"Tell me something Cobb, Missy, she's—"

"One hot gear on a cold clutch; you won't last boy, none of 'em do."

"None of who do you mean, exactly?"

"They'd all a one get back in the saddle they could, ceptin her husband."

"Husband!? Cobb, when you knew she had the hots, you should have warned me!"

"I'll bet she's pretty nice, ain't it, what I always heard."

"You should have said something—another man's wife!" Cobb leered.

"They say that ass got no quit in it."

"A married woman!"

"What they say, they say she's—"

"What am I going to do now!"

"Don't think on it and just keep on a-pumpin' it"

"He threatened me, Cobb."

"Shoot, that boy won't do a thing."

"It's still adultery anyway."

"Listen, when he switched over, she left him so ain't no worrying change a thing. I see you don't get it. Try this: he'd rather have him a foot-long dog than a taco."

"So, they're divorced then?"

"It didn't get to a judge, but why she's shakin' it in his face ever night is easy to see." Separated then, but it wasn't much of a relief: the menace he sensed in Doug was too vivid to ignore, and Randal knew he would have to be careful, yet he didn't *feel* for Missy; she was so bland out of bed as to seem a weightless space in the box of his romantic ideal. Then he heard it, a sort-of ideal, not unlike a bee on a beeline but growing louder until he was jerked from turmoil by a sound that was music to his ears: he stood as it grew ever louder until it burst upon him with a roar and a leather-clad Elmer kicked the bike to its stand and sat there grinning.

2

Merle Terrell sat at the three-legged kitchen table at the weathered family homestead, a hardscrabble farm of buildings leaning like trees in the wind. His fingers ached, and as he soaked his pen hand in a bowl of warm vinegar, he wrapped the other around a fifth of Rebel Yell. He'd been writing letters for a week. He knew that if you didn't yell at 'em, they'd walk all over you. His good for nothing grandson could have helped, but he'd heard nothing, and he was tired of calling over there anyway. Every time it was the same old shit. You'd think he was calling the Pentagon the way that red-haired pit bull answered the phone. Well, it don't matter no more, we done joined forces now and everybody's gonna take orders from me.

He picked up the letter and read it again, even though by now he'd got it memorized. I'll take it over tomorrow when I see Sweenie, and he took a swig from the bottle. I sent all them letters to Raleigh; probably won't a one of 'em help out. They know what they want, and they think they gonna get it, but they don't know us Terrells. He looked again at the letter with the red and white logo of the North Carolina Department of Transportation that stared at him like a bloodshot eye and thought to hell with tomorrow. In the barn he saddled up his horse and made off for the militia compound, and when he cantered up to the farmhouse Sweenie's lip-curled three-legged canine careened around the corner of the house until the choke chain yanked it up short. Sweenie rolled out of bed and was out on the porch in a flash.

"Reagan! Down boy!" The mongrel retreated, chain scraping against the brick of the foundation.

"Didn't know they made that stuff in camouflage," said the older man.

"They're warm," was all Sweenie could think to say, regarding his underwear. Terrell glanced at the sky and sniffed the breeze like a hound.

"Sure is," he said. Indeed, it had dawned unseasonably warm, to some a blessing in the mountains in the fall.

They went inside, and over coffee and donuts they worked out the final arrangements of their covenant. This was precisely what a militia was needed for, contemplated Sweenie. It has settled here upon me like a laurel wreath, the mantle of a knight, and I will honor such commitment to the best of my duty. Little did it matter that the interference was from a state government and not his sworn enemy, the Feds. He rationalized that it might even be for the better: show them at the state and local level that they can't push you around. It serves notice on the big boys that there's a new kid on the block. There weren't going to be any more Wacos, and this wasn't as complex an issue; Terrell didn't claim to be the messiah. The old man went out to check on his horse, and Sweenie admired the gutsy iconoclast. Could have driven over in five minutes, instead he rides his horse along the ridge, shows up like some grizzled cowhand.

He picked up the letter. The North Carolina Department of Transportation would be putting a highway through Terrell's land, one that would give PeeDee County greater access to the interstate currently being gouged to the northeast. Terrell wasn't about to give up his land and had vowed to fight. The square acreage, given one could trust the government maps, comprised roughly ten percent of the county. Thus, the old man, with Sweenie's militia in the van, had determined to secede from the union and with as little dickering as fanfare they had formed The Republic of 1/10 of PeeDee County. Sweenie felt it was too great a mouthful, too much to put on a flag, but he'd salute Terrell's snot rag if it came down to it. His idea of the jamboree had been born of the desire to attract other militia groups to the cause, generate some choice publicity, and strengthen the bastion of freedom. Terrell came back in. "That's some dog you got there: gets around pretty good just three legs."

"Reagan doesn't look like much, but he's fierce," said Sweenie.

"Named him after yer favorite president, did you?"

"On the contrary: I named him after our worst president, that is until that billionaire jackass, but people are too willing to forget how he robbed us blind, bankrupted the savings and loan industry, and ruined thousands of small businesses with his perverse sense of economics. The trickle-down went up, toward the rich. He pissed on everyone else, there's your trickled down.

He was the anti-Robin Hood, steal from the poor and give to the—"

"Son, yer preaching to the wrong man, I don't like none a them," said Terrell.

Sweenie smiled and said he could really go cross-eyed on some topics, and that he'd been living on the street in the eighties when the two-bit actor and the dragon lady had ruled the roost, and he'd been smart enough to see what was happening by reading between the lines: Media kissed White House butt so sweetly their ink had turned brown. Those days made me what today I am.

After they drew up what Terrell said was a contract but Sweenie called a charter, the old man rode back to his home in the woods. Sweenie sat and pondered the historic moment. A citizen whose personal property was suddenly threatened with seizure by the State had enlisted the support of pure patriots to fight Big Brother. And I command the troops! He sat awhile relishing as the ranks began to arrive from their various day jobs, and then he got to work putting together an article for publication, with Randal acting as his agent. Writing had awakened in him a slumbering giant, although as a student he'd disliked it, and had struggled to crank out those essays on the ethics of panhandling and the ecclesiastical nature of begging. Even so, he'd gotten an 'A' for a paper titled, "Brother Can You Spare a Dime: Inflation in the Welfare State." His fondest memory of those grueling hours in the public library was of a biographical essay he'd written on the life and times of San Francisco's most famous street urchin, "Black Jack' Danser, who rose from a Tenderloin rag picker to one of the captains of industry along with Hearst, Stanford, and McDonough and had sculpted California in his image.

The troops had arrived and lined up for roll call, and as Sergeant Stratt was calling the roll, Mr. Terrell again appeared at the edge of the woods. He sat his horse and gazed at the bunch lined up beneath the flagpole in the yard. He'd already met two of them, the Funderbarke brothers. Although he didn't think they had the light on all the time, he was withholding judgment: you can't always tell with mountain folk. That fact alone gave them some leeway and now he observed them again from his vantage point at the tree line. Legroy and Adelroy were twins, and looked it, although Legroy was technically older for having been born one minute and twelve seconds before his brother. Terrell sat his horse and reviewed what he knew of these boys, defenders of North America's second republic.

The brothers Legroy and Adelroy Funderbarke had grown up in Smarmer's Mill, an Appalachian foothill town of ten thousand, where the industry was textiles with a smattering of tobacco and poultry farms set amid the piney crags. The Funderbarke homestead had begun as a hog farm, expanded into tobacco, and during the last half-century had become the final resting place of a hundred head of auto.

Over time the clan evolved into renaissance motorheads, raised up in the garages of Funderbarke Auto Salvage, but they never gave up on tobacco; dirt paths that snaked through the rusting pride of Detroit and Tokyo were tilled for rows of bright leaf. To retrieve a flywheel from an '87 Electra, you had to be a skilled furrow hopper; likewise, to pick tobacco without scraping your knuckles required the poise of a seasoned planter.

The homestead, an antebellum steamboat gothic, had been converted into a garage when the growing junkyard needed an office, mechanic's bays, and storage bins. Leon and April Funderbarke never liked the queer old house anyway, what with its stained glass, gingerbread trim and a widow's-walk between the turrets. Initial improvements included covering the tongue and groove white cypress floors with linoleum and painting the cedar wainscot turquoise. They were determined to live in splendor, not squalor. The house sat well back from Ebenezer Van Hoy Church Road under an awning of Walnut shade trees and hedged by rusting appliance wrapped in wild blackberry swarmed with kudzu.

It was into this semi-urban scene that the Funderbarke twins were raised. The first-born was named for a battlefield decoration of their oldest mechanic, a French national, whose war stories of heroics with the Resistance often preceded the display of his prized possession. "Le Croix de Guerre," he proudly announced. Leon had seen it a hundred times and didn't much care for the dogwah part but thought *Legroy* was a great name. The second boy (April always thought of him as the split-second boy) was named for her brothers Adel and Roy, as the two were as inseparable as her sons would come to be.

As the blond haired, blue-eyed boys grew, they trained too, and became top-notch auto mechanics, but when they learned what their father intended to pay them as employees, they hit the road, finally landing at Ralph's Full Auto in Bluff, an hour northwest where they made contact with the world of the paramilitary: conspiracy theorists, blinded patriotism, and shithouse philosophy. Ralph's Full Auto took on a whole new meaning one day when their boss showed them how to file the sear off a semi-automatic rifle and turn it into a machine gun.

They had both been the first to join the newly formed Tax Resisters And Southern Heroes, but had failed to advance in the ranks because they would listen to each other long before, or after, anyone else. Sergeant Stratt despised them for their reckless approach to discipline, for their clowning and their lackadaisical attitude to authority. Nonetheless, the twins somehow held the others together. Now, as Terrell observed the roll call, he noted that the tow-headed boys had their boots on backwards as they goose-stepped up the driveway. He turned his horse and cantered away.

~ ~ ~

The air was cooler than in the foothills, but still remarkably warm for March. You could usually count on a warm spell about this time anyway, but leather never stopped a cold wind, so Randal and Elmer hauled their bikes in Peaches where they ogled the born-for-bikes switchbacks and fought down feeling silly. They passed through Bluff; a village built on terraced ledges that provided spectacular views of the aptly named Blue Ridge Mountains. Four miles outside of town on a road Randal knew, the old highway veered away from the newer one and crossed a stream before it climbed steeply through switchbacks so sharp a snake would meet its tail before leveling off where again it crossed the stream, and just beyond the second bridge and sitting close up to the road was the farmhouse that now served as the headquarters for the militia group, a newly installed flagpole fluttering a large white banner with purple lettering that read: THE REPUBLIC OF PEEDEE COUNTY in the top half of a radius, and rounding out the disk along the half-circle of the bottom edge were these words: TAX RESISTERS AND SOUTHERN HEROES; in the center a hand painted 1/10, though out of scale, said it all. Grounded beneath the flag were many cars and trucks.

Commandant Sweenie greeted the two warmly. "Have a good trip? I'm glad you made it."

Randal, eyeing the flag said, "The logo you sent said, 'special heroes.'"

"We changed it to better reflect the cause," said Sweenie.

"The coming congrelation," said a young man who'd just joined them. Sweenie chuckled. "Randal, Elmer, like you to meet my chief scout, Legroy Funderbarke."

They shook hands as Legroy ogled Elmer's chaps; he'd never seen anything like leather pants and it was only after Randal and Elmer unloaded the motorcycles from the truck that he understood.

"Hey Legroy, you seen my brother, where's he at?"

"Him and the Buggs are stringin barbwar up to the fort."

Elmer straddled his chopper and jumped on the starter pedal. Ten minutes later it throbbed to life and sat thug-thugging as he wiped the sweat out of his eyes, it was then he noticed Legroy.

"You know why they call it a Harley?" he asked.

Legroy gave the answer proudly, as though repeating the sacred rites of the motorhead creed, but appended it, saying that he knew why, and appended that with a screed on the newer bikes with their electric starters and how that sissy way out had ruined it for many. Randal, not up for the workout, pushed his bike onto the sidewalk and propped it on the side stand as Elmer roared away up the road.

Sweenie gave Randal a tour of the house. In the office there was a computer, a Xerox machine, and a desk. He had expected more, but he noted a diploma given to Sweenie for outstanding service as editor of "*Street-Smart: A Magazine of Outdoor Living.*" On a table sat a stack of newly printed booklets with plastic spiral bindings.

"Ah, I see you've found my group's latest achievement," said Sweenie. He picked up a copy and fanned the pages.

"A must read for every new recruit, like their Bible, you know what I mean." He clapped a hand on Randal's shoulder as he left the room and Randal picked up a booklet and paged through the T.R.A.S.H. Patriot Training Manual. He'd check it out later, but first he was headed for Republic land to meet the troops. He slipped the manual in his pocket and left the house.

They drove from the yard and went up and down trails no wider than Sweenie's vintage Willys until they turned into a rutted dirt track off of the State Road and plunged down a steep embankment before leveling out on a broad meadow that rose again to thick timber on two sides. "Welcome to the Republic of One Tenth of PeeDee County," said Sweenie, in the voice of an announcer. The militia and Elmer were sitting on the ground eating from bag lunches. The Commandant introduced Randal to the troopers one at a time, and by rank.

There was Eddie, grandson of the President of the Republic, and a Captain, who he'd first met at Elmer's and the latter's brother, Buster, whose head, shaped like an inverted iron, bristled with the quills of a freshly crew cut Lance Lieutenant. Randal recalled the photo of the two of them and the bikes and the pretty woman, so unlike Sergeant Lynette, the strangest looking woman he had ever seen; she had no curves, and she seemed to read him with a sneer as he and Sweenie moved on down the line. The next bunch was, when not on active duty, the Pyrates Motorcycle Gang, which was comprised of three groups of brothers, all Privates. In their olive drab duds, Randal couldn't tell them apart, and soon forgot about them. And lastly there were the inseparable Funderbarke twins who sat back-to- back, Adelroy spooning a can of Chef Boyardee and flipping the meatballs over his head as Legroy sought to catch them in his mouth.

"Where's the President?" asked Randal.

"Any idea?" Sweenie asked around. Eddie Terrell shrugged as he ate. They had been stringing barbed wire, and Randal noticed that their fatigues were ripped and torn, not one of them was without a scratch. Sweenie rubbed his jaw and counted again. "Where's Dewit?" he asked.

"Went off to slice him a loaf, probably got lost," said Eddie.

"There he is," said Lester.

Everyone looked across the valley where a tiny figure could be seen thrashing about in thickets.

"What in hell's he doin' way over there?"

"Looking for his brain."

"He ain't gonna find it."

They all stood and yelled, waving their arms. The figure began moving in their direction. Adelroy now stood beside Randal, nodding toward the approaching figure.

"That there's Dewit. Cain't nobody remember his last name, cluding him; we just call him 'Do it.' That's all you got to say you want something done."

"Corporal Funderbarke," said the Commandant.

"Yes sir."

"Why don't you and your brother show our guests the rest of the perimeter?"

Before long they stood at the edge of a ravine overlooking a creek that meandered through deadfall and into a swamp. Randal hadn't known that you could have a low-lying swamp in the mountains and said so.

"That bottom was way bigger before. They filled it in with the bodies of soldiers and old guns and stuff," said Legroy.

"They say there's a whole regiment a Yankees in there, too," added Adelroy.

"How did they get a whole regiment in there?" asked Randal.

"Don't matter. No what else in there?"

"Tell me."

"Woolybooger."

"What?"

"The Woolybooger lives in there."

Randal's eyes went wide as he remembered high school tales of the mythical beast; it was urban; it was primal; it was ageless; it was a teller's talisman, a campfire regular.

"I've heard of that, like Big Foot," he said.

"Hell, that's a Yankee ape. This here's home grown," said Legroy.

Randal surveyed the eerie quagmire as dead tree branches rattled like hollow sticks in the breeze. Down in the bog nothing moved or tittered or sang.

"They say it isn't an ape, though," said Randal.

"How can you tell?" challenged Adelroy.

"Well, they say—"

"*They* is the government, friend, you think they got the answer? That could be the Lindbergh baby for all you know," said Legroy.

"No, he was killed."

"They *say* he was."

The three of them walked along the crest, eyeing the murky fastness below. Although none of them was aware of it at the time, two thirds of Merle Terrell's land was as identical topography, and about as valuable.

"Why does he live in there?" asked Randal.

"Cause he's smart," said Legroy.

Randal thought about that for a moment, awaiting further explanation. "How did it get in there in the first place?"

"It coulda moved," answered Adelroy.

"Why the hell would it move?" challenged his brother, who considered himself the smarter twin.

"Animals do that." They glared at each other.

"Name one," said Legroy.

"Birds," said Adelroy, "they fly south."

"Then why ain't these birds ever leave?" sneered Legroy.

"This *is* the south, dumbass!" and they grappled, twice nearly tumbling over the precipice, and then as though by a hidden signal, stopped. Dripping spittle and spitting blood, sweat streaked faces roughed, they continued the tour. Randal had so far seen a lot of woods, much of it bordering the seemingly endless bottom. They came across small meadows and these pockets opened to the sky and greeted them with dazzling blue. Legroy was saying how they'd plant booby traps in these clearings nearest the road; make the enemy take the long way where the forces of T.R.A.S.H. would be waiting. They emerged from a sizable patch of stinkweed into the bivouac where the troops stood around shooting the bull, having finished their work. Randal asked where Mr. Terrell lived.

"I'll tell you later," snapped Sweenie, who then blew a whistle: "Search and Destroy! Search and Destroy! One Niner Alpha!"

Scrambling, the troop extracted from their field packs handfuls of plastic army men before deploying block and hammer tactics through the grass and Jimson weed enfilade. Before long, they had formed a rough circle and were making shooting noises and explosion sounds. Elmer and Randal, mouths agape, exchanged looks, before turning their attention back to the militia. Randal was on the verge of joining in the fun when Sweenie clicked a stopwatch and yelled "Cease fire!" He turned to his guests.

"I can see you have questions. What you got to understand is that the concept's the same. So are the principles and the tactics. This way everybody gets to see the big picture and how it works. You learn from these practices and by God, you're ready for a well-regulated militia." The troop then headed for their HQ.

Elmer offered his buddy a lift on the Harley and again parked it in front of the house.

"Man, I can't believe it," said Elmer, removing his helmet. "Imagine what would happen if I was to do a re-enactment like that: they'd have me in the nut house so fast I'd piss backwards; I wouldn't know whether to fart or go cross-eyed."

Randal figured there was a catch and dug the training booklet out of his back pocket: page one offered instructions on how to build a pillow fort with a schematic of an inverted U, and he remembered making just such a fort in his room. The next page detailed instructions on how to assemble and disassemble a leaf and stick fort, and his skepticism vanished as he time-traveled back to the leaf fort he and his friends had made for their pea shooter battles, and then he became more engrossed in the booklet: how to make a slingshot, how to enfilade an anthill, but he was interrupted and asked to make a beer run, so he grabbed Elmer and they drove Peaches into town. Upon their return they found their motorcycles had been disassembled and now sat in small piles on the sidewalk. Elmer was speechless. Randal demanded to know what was going on.

"We just had to see how they come apart," said Adelroy.

"All pistons got personality," added Legroy, "no two the same. Yours," he pointed a wrench at Elmer, "gots an ugly disposition, but Randal's sweet as buttermilk."

"Don't worry, we put 'em back together they gonna be a lot happier than they was," stated Adelroy. Since coming to the militia group, the twins had repaired everything that came with moving parts with the exception of Reagan, who was beyond help. Later, Elmer about had a fit when his bike started on the first kick.

Several other militia groups showed up that evening and a huge party ranged around the bonfire, but Randal soon became listless, having heard the noun *guns* ten thousand times. Outside of the circle of fire the air was cold, and he realized with dismay that his chances of finding a beer were slim, but he strolled over to the porch where the Pyrates bike gang was hanging out, changed out of their fatigues into jeans and motorcycle boots, as well as the sleeveless denim jacket that featured the club logo, a one-eyed buccaneer with a knife in his teeth. Randal sat down.

"What kind of bikes y'all got?" he asked.

"Well, we ain't got 'em yet, but we're gonna get 'em, ain't that right boys?" and the others high fived. Randal now understood why they all rode together, crammed into a Subaru station wagon.

"I gots 700 dollars saved," said one.

"Well, how about Pyrates, where did y'all get the name?"

"Well, see they was Rebs like us, and they was smarter than the government."

"Well, they weren't smart enough to avoid getting killed," said Randal, "like Blackbeard, for example."

The other had the facts at his fingertips, however, and fired another salvo:

"That wasn't Blackbeard was killed on the Outer Banks, was his double. All big Pyrates had doubles what could fight for 'em while they was laid up getting some poontang."

Randal laughed also and thought of Missy Rose in her underwear and yearned for Bessboro; there weren't any women up here, unless you counted Lynette, and she was built like a door: a closed one. As he gazed at the bonfire, he tried to imagine sleeping with her but was saved from the image by that of Reagan, licking his balls by firelight. Then his thought line shifted to the newspaper column. How am I going to tell Coleman? How do you fire somebody? The thought conflicted, but he shifted gears to warmer feelings as he imagined his father on stage naked as a jeering audience lobbed rotten fruit. Then he knew: you step up and do it! Elmer nudged him from his reverie with a quart bottle of beer just as a white van pulled into the driveway, WTVF written on the side, and on the roof a satellite dish aimed at the heavens. Grasping the moment, the Pyrates straightened their duds, and Lester conducted his band.

"C'mon," said Elmer, nodding toward a woman with a microphone, trailed by a cameraman, "let's get famous," and they headed for the driveway, the fire a halo beyond.

The following morning Elmer rode shotgun on the trip back to Bessboro. He liked riding up front where you could see everything but not have to drive, knowing his bike was snugly in the back. For that matter, you could damn well drink. Being a beer man, he didn't care for whiskey, but he'd seemingly gargled it the night before and had passed out next to the fire, only to come awake with a jolt and find himself smoldering and then lurched and hopped and howled and awakened the camp. In the morning light he discovered that the hair on one side of his head was singed to the scalp and his face burned in places from the metal frames of his glasses. He was hung over, smelled of stale beer and burnt hair and couldn't see a thing, unable to wear his glasses without crying. He took another pull at his wake-up bottle.

"Listen," said Randal, "we get back to Bessboro this guy Cobb can fix you up: he's got all these country recipes and stuff. One time, Rose, Missy Rose, you know, she got stung by fire ants. They got in her bra when she was out on the stage and when she got dressed, they had themselves a nipple picnic," he said, as he recalled the screams that brought him running.

"What happened?" asked the wild-eyed Elmer.

"Cobb made up this poultice goo and put it on her, had all this stuff in it like okra and rabbit tobacco and we packed it in a bra and strapped it on her and I swear all that guacamole sliding down her belly made me horny as a goat," and he went on with the tale in the belief it would cheer his sullen companion but before long Elmer was snoring a rhythm to the white lines dashing before them and Randle, true to his friend with the burned hair and blackened face and wheezing, snuffling breath, and to the ongoing story in his head, imagined that he was moving the Woolybooger to another swamp.

3

Aaron Salmon's excitement pedaled the exercise bike; he had discovered that he worked well here, that the exercise of the body was also good for the mind was an established fact, and now he had met it face to face. As he pedaled, he explored the parameters of his latest inspiration. This thing could be the next big wave, and not just for Capitol foods. This could definitely be a hit, and he giggled as he estimated the sales that could rescue them from the edge of the red and return them to the black. The more he thought about it the faster he pedaled. We can do it; I know we can do it. How much would we have to sink into R&D?' His breath was coming now in short gasps, and as his heart raced his legs were flying and so was his brain. I'm so sure of this I'll risk my neck. He slowed the bike to a steady pace and then climbed off the machine, giddy with excitement and bright ideas.

If he'd gone to the Kroger with his wife, he would have missed it altogether (not too unlike his intro to Sow Syrup), the news told of an exciting story breaking just over the state line in a small North Carolina town. A militia group that held four thousand acres of mountain land had declared it a republic and seceded from the union. They were demanding recognition from the department of State as well as from the cartographers at Rand McNally. Salmon had listened to the on-scene interview with the group's leader and among the people milling about in the background Salmon thought he recognized one who waved at the camera. The anchor reported that so far there had been no official response.

Early the next morning, Salmon drove up the Shenandoah Valley, resplendent in its spring attire and wondered how many people were on the road not going anywhere, just out for a drive in the beauty, and he sought to imagine the valley without roads; how alluring it must have been to traverse it on horseback. He crossed the North Carolina line and headed southwest, and in Bluff, an aptly named cliff-face hamlet, he got directions to the T.R.A.S.H. headquarters and before long was standing on the porch and ringing the bell. A young man dressed in jungle olive and desert taupe answered the door.

"Sup," he said.

"I've eaten, thank you. Is Mr. Sweenie available?" asked Salmon.

"He's gone to check up, him and Sergeant Bitch."

"I don't mind waiting," he said, and the boy closed the door. Salmon sat on the porch swing and perused his Richmond Times-Dispatch, but unable to focus he put the paper down and looked at his watch. As he did so he saw the face of the young man staring at him through a bay window. Salmon returned the stare before returning to his paper, but he had a hard time concentrating, overcome with curiosity to know if those blond headed ice-blue eyes were still there. He turned to an interview with the Chief Justice, got about three sentences and couldn't bear it, and peeked around the edge of his paper relieved to find no eyes. Then the Chief Justice was describing his favorite brand of American potato salad when a finger slid over the top of the paper and Aaron nearly leapt out of the swing.

"Hey mister," said the young man, holding forth a cup of coffee.

"Why, thank you," said Aaron, folding his paper.

"You reading about that school shooting?"

"Yes, I did, it's very disturbing," said Aaron, taking a sip.

"It's just kids with guns, what's a big deal?"

"When I was a kid," he replied, "you got harassed and you harassed back; it was part of adolescence. Now—"

"Now you better watch your ass," said the boy, working a finger in his ear.

"Well, that's what I'm saying; this new concealed weapons law is making us far less friendly to each other. Do you see this?" asked Aaron.

"What I see is ever man has got a right to protect himself."

"From who?"

"Everbody that's got a gun, that's who," answered the kid, now examining the wax on a fingernail.

"But if everybody has a gun, how do you tell the good guys from the bad guys?"

"Well, you mind your own business, what you do."

"My point exactly: don't smile, don't wave, don't say anything at all to people you don't know," said Aaron, who added, "if a stranger asks for directions, shoot him."

"It ain't that way," said the boy, sitting on a porch rail. He pulled a green yoyo from a cargo pocket and began to bob it as they talked.

"Not yet, I'd say, but that's where we're headed because the Constitution allows every man, woman, and child to own anti-tank weapons, hand grenades, and nerve gas," said Aaron, again hoping the sarcastic approach would kindle a fire in the lad.

"Now yer making fun of the Constitution," said the boy as he walked the dog.

"Believe me, I am not. I'm just afraid for us all. I believe that good people deserve better from each other than the suspicion and distrust that are promoted through the encouragement of deadly force." He sipped his tepid coffee. "But as an American, I shouldn't have to fear other Americans."

"You just gotta be faster on the draw," said the young man. Aaron gave up. The boy just wasn't listening, was he? He's so completely sold on the weapon plan that he can't see beyond it. Unwilling to give, he framed another angle.

"The Constitution guarantees your rights, but we all need to be responsible in our exercise of those rights."

"It's what the Constitution don't say that's important to us," said the kid, as a jeep pulled into the yard and Commandant Sweenie swung over the side, thereby saving the marketer from the bog of further discussion with Legroy Funderbarke.

Later, as he drove back down the Shenandoah Valley, he again took in its scenic majesty, from the budding dogwoods by the roadside to the purplish sweep of the distant peaks and was reminded that this valley was one of the reasons old Bob Lee had taken up the sword against his fellow Americans. Pretty, yes. But not pretty enough to kill for; the only killing worth the time and sweat is like the one I just made, one that will re-establish the name of Capitol Foods as preeminent, known in every home in the land, and he congratulated himself for making the right moves: so far, so good. From his initial email, his wife, a commercial artist, had designed a mock-up of the new product. What he liked about it was that there was no gun. That sent a message right there, and Sweenie had reinforced it when he'd told him: this isn't about guns or the NRA, it's about rights and governmental abuse. Next, Aaron would use his creative powers to write the slogan for the back of the package and he flicked his gaze to his attaché case which held the print.

~ ~ ~

Aaron Salmon pitched his idea with all the gusto he could muster, applying his three-color charts and tables for affect, in the Capitol Foods conference room. Though on familiar ground as a team player presenter and marketer, this time he felt like he was flying by the seat of his pants when the finale of the presentation was met by silence, and that meant only one thing. He began to put away his display when the company president shot out of his chair.

"It's brilliant, absolutely brilliant! Patriotism always sells apple pies and turkey dinners! I can see them lining up for this cereal, the newest brand from Capitol

Foods," and he seemed to dance for a minute, his bald spot glistening as the manifestation of a great idea.

"Breakfast, it's the most important meal, healthy," and on he went, ticking off items on his fingers, "get you going like a patriot!"

"Sir," said a junior ad executive.

"Yes?"

"How about the slogan: 'The Crunch Heard Round the World.'"

The silence this time was measured by whispering air ducts as the boss put his arm around Aaron and the two men marched from the room like comrades reunited. They would begin production immediately and Aaron found himself in a whirlwind of orders, proclamations, and directives, like a commanding general before a battle. He also found himself, much to his surprise and disgust, smoking a cigar as he and the president gazed out the office window at the Richmond skyline.

"Militia-Man Cereal."

"Yes, Militia-Man Cereal, it has a ring to it that isn't forced, that rolls off the tongue. It'll be its own advertisement in a way, not that we're going to hold back that bronco: we'll hit them with both barrels. Now, about the coupons," and the two of them hunkered down to hammer out the details.

The Sow Syrup pitch, now a seeming trifle, was forgotten, as it seemed to have also been with Randal who felt like a man in charge of his own destiny, and as soon as he got out of hock to L.D. he'd decide on whether to remain in Bessboro, move to the mountains, live at Elmer's, or beneath the magnolias at the Ramseur mansion. It seemed to him that he was always flying between re-enactments, hogs, and militia, but he missed Raleigh. He liked going back and hanging out, as long as he didn't have to see his father.

He had planned to head back there the next day, when this thing came up. Frankly, he didn't want to work all weekend; shoot, he didn't want to work at all, what he wanted was to lie in bed with Missy Rose, even if she did have that stupid dog with her now wherever she went. Well, who bought the stupid dog, huh? Shopping in Raleigh, he'd taken her out to the malls where, counter-intuitively given her line of work, she had spent hours putting on clothes. Then, strolling past a pet store she just had to have that Yorkie in the window, and a cutie pie it was until they rolled; the thing had barked the whole way back to Bessboro, giving Randal a taste of things to come. He'd tried to drown it out with some country tapes Elmer had given him, but he couldn't decide which was worse, the dog's incessant yip or the yippee-ay-o-kayay; he'd tried Metallica but barks between the beats was more awful yet.

Their relationship had begun wantonly enough: she took him to bed one night, half- dressed after a show, after the lights and glares had dimmed, when for her his innocence was a beacon of freshness, a new amber spotlight against the trucker culture cat-call darkness of every other night at the motel café-nightclub, and he folded into that role like a cameo.

They were a newly coupled couple whose passion turned the gears of romance in the heat of the moment but otherwise left them edgy and confrontational. Randal mused: all we ever do is get naked and contort, but otherwise before and after we're dullards for each other. That's romance? As she was the elder, Randal felt he had a lot of catching up to do but wasn't at all sure he had what it took for the long run. So far, the token gambit he'd accepted as love seemed a bit manufactured, like a strip-tease act it drew you in breathlessly, and then the stage went dark. These thoughts mingled with his mom's recent remarks and chewed within him as he drove out to the sump to meet up with Cobb.

"Got a problem thonny, thith here thing done grown, lookee here," and he led the way past the sump and its droning pump where beneath the burm of the waste lagoon there burbled and spat a brown morass of vile, smelly goo. Cobb showed him how the new fissure had all but obliterated the smaller.

"We could handle that other flow," said Cobb, who saw a problem and a way out as the same: well, it doesn't really matter, does it? Some of the stuff went right on by them, didn't it? That's what the creek is for, isn't it? It couldn't really be a problem, could it? Randal fielded these questions and though unsure of their answers for a moment or two he held in abeyance the assumption they had nothing to worry about as he drove back to town, except for the nagging, pestering whispers, again that sense that something wasn't right, something unloved, was it the dad thing, was it Missy… god what an appetite, but no… was it something Matilda had said, some warning maybe, something in the tone of a statement, but that wasn't it either and it tugged at him as something bigger than these random guesses, but he couldn't dredge it up and it only did happen when he made light of time; it surfaced because it was impersonal, and coldly so. He turned away from the hamlet and followed the tree line that bordered the creek, and turned again away and then at times running at right angles but keeping the tree line in view until he came back and crossed a little bridge marked Neuse River and saw about a mile away where the two would have to join, and pulling to the side of the road and without another thought he got the number through his Smart phone and made the call.

Dale knew better, of course: 'this here ain't too different from the way it was before when daddy had the farm, and look what happened, feds and state people was all over they ass: threatened to put all us in jail; Shoot, fines so big you couldn't ever pay; Brought in newspapers and even T.V.; Made a big ole stink, and out a what, couple a dead fish; Damn liberals what it was, tree huggers and animal rights folk; Try and ruin a man's life, what he does to feed his family. Well, they had their day, but mine's on a rail. They want be tellin' *me* this time, no sir! They want be in *my* face with their damn regulations this time, no sir, they surely will not!'

~ ~ ~

Missy sat in the Sooweet Dreams Motel & Cafe with a cup of coffee and a cigarette, the Yorkshire terrier on her lap as she batted the breeze with her strip-tease partner.

"Dju get her a name yet?" asked Linda-Lou, a plump woman, her hair up in curlers.

"Well, listen to this: Randal thought it was a boy," she whispered, a laugh deep in her throat. "She's got so much hair he couldn't find her pee-pee, so he just named her Otis!"

"Ewww," said Linda-Lou, "but it ain't no boy dog, any fool can see that."

"I know, and that's why I'm calling her Rose for my stage name. But don't tell Randal. When he's around I call my little baby-wayby Otis Rose and he likes it!"

As if on cue, Randal entered the cafe, and Linda-Lou said she had to get her hair done and left them.

"Hey, listen baby," said Randal, sliding into the booth, "I got to go back to the mountains and work on that article I'm writing about PeeDee County, and I want you to come with me." He hoped to get away from Bessboro and Doug who continued to pop up at odd times. "Honey, I got to make a living," she said, stabbing out her cigarette.

"I'm giving you time off with extra pay. You deserve a vacation. You work your ass off."

"No, honey, I dance my ass off as you should know because that's all you ever see. Try looking me in the eye for a change; this is where the woman is." An hour later they were rolling down the interstate, but Randal was less than jovial. He had envisioned a great romantic getaway, but his ideal of bliss had been chiseled by the tongue lashing that was followed by one from Otis, each yipping screech oddly in time to the beats of every band. He changed the channel on his fantasy and saw himself feeding the dog to Doodlebug and worked on that image and a stick of Juicy-fruit gum as he drove further toward the west.

4

L.D. had spent several hours on the greens at the country club working on his swing. Now, as he relaxed in the lounge, he observed other golfers through the tinted windows. Upon going to the bar for a refill he glanced at the newspaper lying there and returned to the table with the paper and his fresh drink. His man had been right, right on the money, and he had gotten out when the getting was good. The Honeycutts are a sad lot, anyway, he reasoned, this sort of calamity fits their profile like a shadow. He sipped the cold Glenfiddich and licked his lips.

The large reservoirs that collect hog waste are called lagoons as the paper informed. One of the lagoons at Honeycutt Farms located in Bessboro had apparently ruptured. At first a mere trickle had leaked, but a watchful farmhand had pumped it into barrels which had since been confiscated by the Sheriff's department. Unfortunately, the employee had not reported the damaged lagoon, but someone else certainly had. The article, accompanied by a graphic that chronologically detailed the events, went on to relate that as pressure in the lagoon destabilized, the leak had enlarged until the lagoon burst. From an environmental standpoint, it was by far the worst leak of hog waste into a river in the state's history. Not only were fish dying by the thousands, there had also been reports of swimmers emerging with lesions, divers with horrifying port wine welts. L.D. whistled through his teeth, appalled by the news that the governor had declared Bessboro to be a disaster area and was applying for federal emergency aid. In the face of such a monumental debacle, his profit seemed paltry by comparison, and he couldn't stop himself from wondering if there was yet money to be made. As past president of the North Carolina Pork Council, he still had many friends in the industry. Then, another thought struck: I may no longer be able to count on Randal's payments, but perhaps there's another way to play it. Yes, I think there is after all. After supper that night he called the number at which he'd first spoken to Randal.

"What can I do for you," said a gruff voice.

Without identifying himself, L.D. said: "I bought Shives Poe's dress sword from your son." There was silence on the line.

"It wasn't his to sell. It belongs to me."

"Well, that's why I called, sir, I felt that as one gentleman to another we could negotiate its return." L.D. smiled at the thought of another blade swapped in the night; he had many in the collection and he doubted Poe ever so much as glanced at the thing and thus was ripe for a rip off.

"What did you have in mind?" asked Everett Poe. L.D. told him.

"I'd piss on your mother's grave."

"You should talk to your son, he's got quite a lot of money, so I hear," tempted an unruffled L.D.

"That ingrate, don't know where he is," replied Poe, who then heard an offer more fantastic than the first:

"I'll tell you where you can find him, the actual address and phone number, call it a buy-one-get-one once in a lifetime deal for, say, ten Grand," said L.D., striving to be fair and reasonable.

After a measured silence, Poe spoke and the two of them worked out an arrangement, and L.D. knew he'd judged Poe correctly. After all, a mere ten thousand was peanuts. He then called his half-brother with the good news that the confusion over the swords had at last been cleared up.

Also purchasing information that day was the corpulent columnist Tarleton Ramseur. He had 'bought' the name of Coleman Sweenie just as he had done with that of Titus Shell, and for a similar cost. Later, as he and his wife ate supper, he reviewed the entire mess that began with Randal's opening gambit. He sensed a loose cannon in the lad, but one more naive than diabolical, that he didn't intend to keep his word; and who meanwhile kept running headlong into serial events with unsavory endings. The young man needed a guide.

"This man Sweenie, you're going to do something, I can smell it," said Carolotta, amusement in her voice.

"I believe that's hominy, dear," he said.

"I want to interview him, or rather, not as a newspaper man, as my name is somewhat known, but as a friendly dust buster just passing through."

"And how do you propose to carry this off?" She passed him the chicken.

"Bibs, straw hat, farmer tan. Borrow a truck, put me a short dog under the seat," he drawled, for effect.

"Where would Pa Kettle be without Ma?" she asked.

"You could do it! Yes, it's a wrap!" And he rose from the table waving his butter knife like a conductor's baton.

~ ~ ~

The Honeycutts sat in their kitchen hangout remembering better times, and wistfully so the signing party. Dale drank whiskey out of a bottle, and Betty, nose tucked into her blouse, washed it. Gladys was asleep on the couch, blissfully beyond more suffering for one day. While every family member had been hit with the shock wave that knocked them silly, Gladys had taken the brunt of it by what transpired after the deputies arrived.

The first sign that something was awry appeared in the form of a helicopter that circled low and ran the barn rows that ordinary day, but a day like any other got walloped when it hovered. Later a prop plane and then another swooped over the lagoons and before you could sneeze the farm was swarmed with running people, as though a tour had run amok, but tours didn't wear uniforms.

It was just after the bullhorn squelch that Durwood went ape-shit, punched a deputy, grabbed his sidearm, and ran screaming through the pens, shooting into the air. A troop of officers set out after him, but his wild delivery checked theirs and in pandemonium they banged each other, skated in mud, and made flying tackles of air. When he was finally cornered, it took seven deputies to put the cuffs on him, but even then, he was as dangerous as a feral pig. Following a car-top confab of badges, the authorities transferred him not to jail but instead to a State psychiatric facility known euphemistically as Little Dix, as it sat adjacent to

Raleigh's historic and infamous bughouse that currently housed Health and Human Resources. Well, that whole shebang was finally over when their family doctor had given Gladys a sedative and Betty remarked on how badly they all needed one. Doug too had gone to Raleigh, but not under arrest, for he had connections in the capital, but at first, he accompanied the ambulance and its occupant as far as he was allowed, and then he went in search of a lawyer.

The other bad news, well, it was one of those days, wasn't it? The defective lagoon was to be drained into the others, and the excess pumped into sewage trucks. Then, the next lagoon would undergo the same process as state engineers and EPA personnel checked each one for stability. As a result, the hogs were to be put into quarantine. They would be herded and moved gradually so not to overburden the state's meager resources for refugee swine.

~ ~ ~

Randal and Commandant Sweenie rewrote the final stages of the T.R.A.S.H. manual before it went off to the printer, then turned their attention to a new project: the magazine that as yet had no title, but they were considering *The Patriot's Pamphlet.* The inaugural issue would contain a mixture of articles, poetry and prose. Randal felt he had rejuvenated his passion for poetics and figurative language through the writing he'd done for the newspaper; one style of creativity had sparked another, but he seemed to be stumbling now, and turned again to the dog-eared pages of his father's play, *Eros Agonistes.* It had never been published, so he cherished lifting the words and working them. Even so, after reading it twice he couldn't understand why his father thought it was so bad as to be consigned to the attic, for his favorite lines were those of the old Cuban fisherman who related a woeful tale about the greatest fish he had ever caught, only to see it devoured in a feeding frenzy of lesbian mermaids. The fisherman, who instructed the reader to call him Ishmael, said: 'those were the breasts of the times; those were the worsted times, and full of the fury of sounds, harbors signifying nothing.'

Randal laid it aside and turned to an article on the desk. Sergeant Stratt, so much alike his dad's gruff demeanor, had written a surprisingly sensitive expose on the illicit trade in fake pink-poodle-hair-pieces that was threatening to undermine the Appalachian wig industry and ruin the livelihoods of honest, hardworking Americans. Mom would laugh at that, he thought, and missed her then, the flash of a distant beacon, shot through with semaphore dashes of tenderness.

"Let me show you something," said Sweenie, as he left the room and returned a moment later brandishing a cereal box.

"This is *my* writing," he said with a smirk. The front panel of the box of (Vitamin Enriched!) Militia-Man Cereal displayed a G.I. Joe-type character replete with camo fatigues. In one hand he held an American flag, and in the other a bowl of cereal. On the back panel, beneath a color photograph of burning picnic tables was the caption:

One summer at Yellowstone my family mobilized to avoid the hordes of bears and scavenging tourists, and we found a quiet corner of a high alpine meadow. Much to our dismay, we discovered that we were not alone, but had stumbled on an armored recon unit of Russian tanks. Fortunately, we were able to dispatch them thanks to the training we received from our Special Militia-Man Training and Tactics Handbook that we got when we redeemed six box top coupons of Militia-Man Cereal. When my wife said, 'please pass the potato salad,' what she really did was give us a secret attack signal coded for the picnic combat assault. The tanks were destroyed with HE disguised as plastic mustard and ketchup bottles. This could happen to YOU!

Buy this product and help protect your country!

Beneath the caption were the instructions that with only three box-top coupons you could now remove even the toughest camo paint with a jar of Commando Brand Cold Cream.

"This is really something," said Randal. He was impressed with his editor's pizzazz and the breadth of his talent.

"We also adjusted the Training Manual to reflect the cereal, here," and he showed Randal what he was referring to: *How To Field Strip a Cigarette: Hold the tube between your fingers and stroke it level to the plain you hold it on. Swiftly guide your fingers down the shaft and eject the fire from the end. Mash it under your jack-boot (Jack-boots are 16 MM box tops). But remember, recruit, One World Tobacco may be your worst enemy. Note: Roman Artillery was recently spotted at the Indianapolis 500 bearing Marlboro logos. BEWARE! BE ALERT!*

"Coleman, this is totally off the wall, but heady stuff!" cried Randal, as the door opened and Dewit shuffled in.

"Private Dewit request to speak with permission," he mumbled. Randal had never really gotten a close look at the man and appraising him noted he was as strong as an ox but thick as a brick, and a further simile struggled to rise, like the thought process in the sunburned giant who moved with a stoop shouldered, splay footed gait suggestive of someone carrying a heavy weight, as perhaps the way Atlas would appear after a million years of hoisting the globe on his shoulders. As for Dewit, just making sense of the world about him was weight enough. Beneath his slicked black hair, one eye seemed to wander to the left as the other pointed to the right, reminding Randal of that Yogi Berra saying: *when you come to a fork in the road, take it.*

"At ease, Private."

"Sir, Mister Legroy I mean Corprul fixin' to give a letcher."

"Thank you, Dewit, you're dismissed." Soon after, Commandant Sweenie and Randal joined the others gathered around the Funderbarke boys. Legroy was speaking:

"You see that Sun Maid Raisins lady and the Land-O-Lakes butter babe with her tits where her knees oughta be? Them's sisters. You look at 'em sometime, you'll see what I mean. They was drawn by the same guy."

"So, they sisters, so fuckin' what!?" challenged Adelroy.

"Don't you see? Okay, who drawn them pictures?"

"The hell would I know?" answered Dewit, and Legroy smacked him with a stick.

"I ain't asked you—Adelroy?"

"I don't know."

"That's just what I'm saying: don't nobody know! Why you think that's a secret, huh?" he said, slapping his palm with the stick as he paced.

"The government says at stuff's OK to eat, right?"

"I reckon," seconded by nodding heads.

"So, they know morn they saying. Another thing is why them women ain't got names?"

"Why?" said Adelroy and Dewit in unison.

"Well, I don't exactly know, but it damn sure is part of the same caspiracy; I can feel it, like that candy bar, Three Musketeers. Why they three of 'em, you ever think about that?" And, so it went with many topics of interest to the troops. Randal sat with his arm around Missy, her arm around Otis Rose, who kept a wary eye on Reagan, snoring fitfully in the gravel. Since their arrival, Randal and Missy had hiked in the hills on trails as yet undecorated with booby traps, but otherwise sat around the house. One day while she was teaching Otis Rose to walk on her hind legs, Missy looked through the pickets that lined the side porch of the headquarters and saw a big fat man get out of a rust red pickup truck. Randal didn't notice because he was playing hound and sniffing up Missy's barbeque. She swatted him every time she felt his nose between her legs, and they went around the porch like a miniature three ring circus.

"B.J. Vassal, you call me Bob," said the fat man, shaking hands with Sweenie. He was a large pink man in a raggedy straw hat, white T, and faded denim overalls with a corncob pipe stuck out the breast pocket. Beside him a plump, blue-eyed blonde peered over the top of a church fan.

"I'm an auctioneer by trade, but I dabble in many an area: tobacco, history of the peanut, zeppelins, commando gadgetry since the Civil War, and unicycles. When I've the time, I also stick my nose into freelance writing," he narrated, hooking his thumbs in the shoulder straps. Sweenie took a liking to him immediately and based on his world wise experience in such matters, judged him to be an honest man.

"I'm happy that you have taken the time to visit us, sir—"

"Bob."

"To visit us, Bob, how can we help you?"

"Saw the news about y'all, thought maybe I could sell me a story to the real media, you know, like *Argosy, American Hunter, Reader's Digest.* But also, I just, well, me and the little woman, we just wanted to shake your hand."

"Please," said Sweenie, gesturing, "be my guests," and they went up the steps and into the house and were given the grand tour and the more Tarleton saw the more expansive he became, and the wider he ranged the more quickly he discovered his host to be an asocial sycophant. Carolotta mostly just smiled, said little, and trailed along behind the jabbering men, but she was getting it all on tape, the recorder snug inside her plastic fishnet handbag.

Later, when they were treated to a lunch of BLT's on white bread with tea, Tarleton was so excited over the surprise of his favorite dinner sandwich that he nearly let the horses out of the barn.

"What newspaper is that?" said Sweenie, who held a glass of tea with a big yellow smiley face on it.

"Excuse me?" said Tarleton, as Carolotta kicked him again.

"You just said the newspaper you worked for would love a story like this. I thought you said you freelanced," said Sweenie.

"Ho ho, oh my, oh yes," said Tarleton, his mind racing.

"I used to edit a small paper, little mountain town of Larry's Knob, Tennessee. Let's see, that must have been, yep, couple years out from Journalism, my major at Mars Hill," he said, occupying his face with the sandwich in hopes of hiding behind it, but Sweenie went right on with the dialogue, suspecting nothing and sensing less.

"If you folks would care to stick around a little longer, our chief scout is ready to make his latest report."

"Why thank you, sir," said Tarleton, "we are much obliged to your hospitality." They weren't introduced to all the ranks, but as Carolotta would later remark, the ones they met were rank enough, and at the top of the list was Corporal Legroy Funderbarke.

Since the initial newscast at the T.R.A.S.H. jamboree, there had been a blitz of media. On any given day there had been journalists knocking, and the phone hadn't stopped ringing. Even now there was a camera crew setting up across the road. The effect of all this on Legroy no one could have guessed, as it had turned a soft-spoken feckless pinhead into a bumptious bumpkin. But for all of his arrogance and comic mockery, Sweenie kept him around because he was simultaneously an idea man and a yes man, the ace adjutant.

As a measure of his status as a rising star in the T.R.A.S.H. hierarchy, Legroy had souped up his wheels and glued a set of Texas longhorns to the hood of his Jeep, and on the roof, he installed a red bubble light from a 1957 Chrysler police car, flanked by fog lights and a small forest of antennae. The newly accoutered vehicle was further equipped with L.L. Bean camo-curtains, over-sized double-wall tires fitted with Mag wheels and on the back a bumper sticker: *I Love My Country but Fear My Government.*

Dressed now in lizard skin cowboy boots, bloused desert battle fatigues, and an Eisenhower jacket striped with naval chevrons, he paraded in front of his truck with his swagger stick, a hickory sapling whittled to a spear point at one end for roasting marshmallows, tucked under his arm as he presented his latest finding to the troops and guests who sat before him on folding chairs.

He had been convinced for some time, he told them, that road signs and highway markers were either spelled backwards or upside down and contained coded messages for invasion forces. On scouting missions, he would stop on the side of a highway and stand on his head to read the mile markers. Sometimes he would also employ a detached rear-view mirror with a flip switch for night work, but using the mirror was probably the hardest part of his undercover work, not only had he to maintain perfect vertical balance, but he had to do it one-handed, keeping the other one free for mirror adjustments.

He decided not to tell his audience about the recent occurrence. He'd been balancing on his head and adjusting the mirror to line it up on a sign that read **ASHVILLE 25,** when an upside-down State Patrolman loomed into view. He tumbled over so fast that he whacked his funny bone and the mirror skidded across the pavement to be crunched by a passing tractor-trailer.

"You look at the sign for **BOONE** one these days," he said, and then advised them not to use a film developing company for security reasons.

"Use Instamatic, you send film in and they gonna disappear you so fast your bones will burn rubber." He paused for affect, gauged by the fear meter of Dewit's face.

"You hold that picture upside down and read it backwards. First, I didn't see nothing, not all signs got 'em, but then I saw how they hide the number 13 in the letter **B**, and damn if it didn't jump out at me like a frog fart."

"Thirteen bad luck," said Dewit, as a shiver ran through him.

"Bad luck ain't the half of it! You see, that sign really says 1300 NE," he said.

"So, what if you ain't got the code book?" said Adelroy. Legroy swacked him with the stick and for a moment they were eyeball to eyeball.

"It don't take a codebook, squirrel brain. What's thirteen-hundred mile northeast a here?"

"Boone?" offered Dewit.

"Ah piss in the hymnal, Boone, moon, it don't matter; I'm trying to tell you they ain't nothing thirteen hundred mile north east a here except the At-fuckin-lantic Ocean! I had to put myself in their shoes." Dewit watched Legroy's boots as he paced, tapping the swagger stick against his leg.

"And then I seen it like Moses and the pillar assault. It ain't thirteen hundred," and he drew the word **BOONE** in the dirt with the stick before rubbing out the vertical bar of the B to expose a 3.

"About then I got so excited I near spoke in tongues. You know what's 300-mile northeast a Boone? Huh? Washington D.C. is what!"

Dewit shot to his feet with a look of pure terror. "Tell the Colonel, tell the Colonel!" he cried.

"We ain't got a Colonel," said Adelroy, easing the big man back into his chair.

Tarleton was jealous that his wife could hide behind her church fan though her shoulders shook; his only defense was biting his tongue.

"You see how serious this is, why I'm doing this here vestigation. Right now, I'm looking at all the North Carolina towns that starts with B, Baden, Bessboro, Bynum, Burlington, but Bat Cave has proved me right. He gathered everyone in a semi-circle before scratching Bat Cave in the dirt. Randal and Missy stood together arm in arm, his skepticism rolling its eyes but his own eyes sweeping her fantastic bod, whereas her concern was Bessboro's imminent invasion.

"Now, everbody walk by on this side," and as they filed slowly by, they saw written in the dirt, **EVAC TA 13**. "You see they got it all planned, and why we need a well-regulated militia."

Driving back home the Ramseurs shared many a good laugh as they retold their favorite parts of the day's activities. For his own part, Tarleton had a hard time believing that the state would put a road through bottomland the likes of which he had seen.

"One thing that strikes me as odd," said Carolotta, "was the absence of law enforcement. There wasn't so much as a security guard keeping watch."

"Honey, you are an eagle eye on a peach blossom. You're right, and that is significant. Some media were there, but local. I happen to know the station manager."

"Do you think Randal recognized us?"

"Not at all: he never had a chance between the attentions of that little lady and the histrionics of the scout. Besides, that lecture had them all spellbound."

"Me too, dear, why, my head is still ringing!"

5

With students headed for the beach and other spring break destinations, Poe mused that very soon would he spring on his son and break his neck, the chiseling prick. That much would be gratifying. Just the thought of it had brought to him such a deep sense of closure that he had willingly paid the ten thousand for the information that the pissant was hiding out in a hamlet down east, that one on the news. Before leaving, he put the shotgun back in the cabinet; perhaps that's a bit rash, he contemplated, as he packed extra whiskey. No, I won't shoot him; that would be too easy. I want to feel my hands on his neck, or maybe the rope in the trunk, string him up, and as he bounced around in ghastly scenarios, he merrily drove away to the truck rental, but he forgot to lock the door.

Poe senior had calculated his every move, examined all the angles and approaches, and then designed a plan. As he drove into Bessboro he began to rehearse his role, think like a trucker, for he'd heard many a director proclaim: don't play the role, assume the character so that you think as one. Poe hadn't written any dialogue, but he'd done everything else. He was driving a rental tractor-trailer, the slatted kind used for hauling livestock, and had labored at practicing the shifting through the multiple gears but as he entered the hamlet there was far less grinding than before, although reverse was a bitch as he parked among a line of similar trucks. Perfect. Then, pouring a cup of coffee from his thermos, thankful that he'd already added the bourbon; he licked his lips and studied his reflection in the mirror. The dyed hair was a shocking blond and the beard looked awful, he realized, but it wouldn't to others. With the cap he felt that he gained an inch. The little rat-fuck will never suspect it. As he drank his coffee, he scanned the odd collection of buildings across the road when a dark-haired woman in a tight skirt left a motel room and entered the cafe. Hot damn! Poe climbed out of the cab and swaggered his way into the Sooweet Dreams to begin the hunt.

As Poe was busy sweet-talking Linda Lou, North Carolina Agriculture officials continued the process of removing thousands of pigs from Honeycutt Farms. The occasional deep-throated blast of a truck horn failed to signal the playwright, already well into Act One of a new drama. Hell, it's a truck stop isn't it? After twenty minutes in the cafe the two of them had spent an hour supine in number eleven. As they dressed, Poe heard repeated horn blasts and pulled aside the curtain: it looked like there was someone in his truck! On the verge of catching Randal, he considered this Herculean effort at dipping his wick to be a part of that measure, and he told her he'd be right back. As he rounded the corner. he ran smack into a State Highway Patrolman.

"Driver, is that your rig?" he said.

Poe noticed that of the many trucks that had been parked across the road, his was now the only one.

"We need to roll on out of here. As arranged, you follow me to the Ag farm," said the patrolman as he got into his car.

What the fuck is this all about, thought Poe. He was about to frame a question when he saw that his truck was packed with snuffling hogs. The State Trooper tapped his horn and pointed down the road.

Several hours later the escort and truck entered the grounds of the North Carolina Agriculture Department Research Station near Sanford, having covered the entire distance at forty-five miles an hour, the emergency flashers of the escort vehicle keeping a steady cadence. As Poe had learned, the state intended to quarantine the pigs until the lagoons had all been drained, examined, tested, and certified as safe. The entire farm would be gone over with an official fine-toothed currycomb until every code requirement was satisfied. Only then would the swine be returned to their pens.

"All right, let's hit it," said the Trooper. "I believe we can make at least two more runs," and he slipped on his mirrored shades, reflecting an unhappy little blond man with a red face.

State officials in their continued sweep of Hogville had removed from the farm dozens of barrels of hog waste from an unmarked metal building, and also confiscated was the bottling operation of some other vile, murky liquid. As the epicenter of all that bad karma, Bessboro was a hive of law and order by day, but by night nothing moved; the bumper cars were parked, the Ferris wheel without motion. Only the tree frogs felt lively enough to serenade a diminishing chorus of oinks in the yard.

Randal was in bed with Missy in her room at the Sooweet Dreams Motel that morning. Since the commotion created by the spill had dissipated, Bessboro had somewhat returned to its original tranquility; the way it had been before the blaring horns and loud music of its heyday as a place on the verge of *happening.* Instead, this morning the lovebirds awoke to a sound greater than squawking police radios: no sound at all. As he peeked through the blinds Randal thought of Legroy's lecture on invasion and wondered if it had been acted out while they slept, and even though he'd dismissed the report as an outlandish if not creative spur of paranoia, the scout was often correct, if by circuitous means. So, what if.... He sank back to bed, to joy and to be joyed, to meld, to suckle and be suckled, but she escaped to a hair problem and he thought, it can't really be happening, the towns that begin with B? When they sneaked a peak an hour on, the village was deserted, and they tossed what they had in Peaches and skedaddled.

Off toward the West, Merle Terrell was also distraught. It just hadn't gone the way he knew it must. He'd expected to be a star, the darling of the media, and the focus of at least one federal agency. He had imagined a communications trailer full of FBI agents working 24hour shifts as they negotiated with him by phone, and his name in the headlines of every major newspaper, spoken of in awe by friend and foe alike, for which he had spent an unusual amount of time in trying to decide what to call himself, other than Merle: *General* was too general and *President* too grand. Sweenie had suggested that they were all guerillas, and when Lynette repeated the word the next day on patrol, Dewit had screamed and run off into the brush.

"Now look what you done," said Adelroy.

The action had so startled her that for a moment she forgot to be tough.

"All I said was—"

"Gorillas, now he's gone think the woods is full of monkeys. It's bad enough we got us the Woolybooger."

"Well, *I* ain't no gorilla," spat one.

"You're ugly enough," said another.

"Well, if we's gorillas what's at make the Commandant?" said yet another, and for the first time since the troop's formation there were murmurs of dissent. They had believed they were equals, excepting Dewit, but now this singular uncertainty had awakened a curious doubt.

Merle Terrell had also begun to doubt. There had been an initial burst of attention in the local news. CBS had sent some people to interview him, but the story had never aired. Weeks had gone by, and nothing. What made it worse was the complete absence of bulldozers. No earthmovers. No dump trucks. No engineers in hard hats and their sissy-yellow carryalls, zilch. He rode his horse out to where his land abutted the state highway where the common vehicle was a Winnebago headed for a Pisgah wildlife adventure and trailing out behind it a serpentine string of sedans.

He'd taken this ride now every day for three weeks. Even his troops conducting live fire exercises deep in the woods had failed to scare up anything more than birds, the ones that got away, that is. Today he was riding another way; down through the woods and bogs to a point where he'd emerge behind the T.R.A.S.H. headquarters. It was time that he and his junior officer, Commandant Sweenie, and his G-2, Chief Scout Funderbarke, had a little talk.

"We gotta shoot somebody," he told Sweenie, as he tied the reins to the porch rail.

"Somebody big," he added.

"Dewit's pretty damn big," suggested Legroy.

"Listen to me boy," and he thumped the scout's chest with a finger, "I'd shoot your sorry ass if I thought it would draw us some attention."

"Your point is well taken, General Terrell. But Tax Resisters And Southern Heroes doesn't just shoot people," said Sweenie.

"Look at Ruby Ridge. Look at Waco: them boys would a starved to death if they hadn't capped a couple Smokies," said Terrell.

"General," said Sweenie, as he came down the steps to stand in front of the old man, "in those cases they were provoked, and they defended themselves. But in our case, so far there has been no provocation."

"That's what the hell I'm tellin' you. We need us a voca—what that word was," said Terrell, rolling a cigarette. Legroy was no help; he hated big words, more than a few syllables and it was a foreign language.

"Well, we might be able to plan some kind of compromise," said Sweenie, stroking his jaw.

"What do you think, Corporal Funderbarke?"

"That horse sure got a big dick," said Legroy, shaking his head.

"Corporal: we need a briefing. Please gather the troop in the yard as soon as they arrive."

Terrell mounted and rode off, saying that he'd return after dark to hear what they had to say. Sweenie knew that to confront the challenge of his commanding officer would be a breach of protocol, but following a conversation with his media rep, Randal, he thought he knew a better way. The kid's journalistic instincts were clicking on all cylinders: promotion in the ranks, he'd said, move everyone up a notch, draw publicity, he'd make a few calls; it'll give those promoted a greater sense of purpose; empower their tarnished vitality. Sweenie then caught the riff and ran with it: this command will uphold the merits of volunteerism and buttress the bonds of camaraderie! Those held at private for so long would make corporal, except for Dewit, but a Pfc. would be considered. Sergeant Lynette had often demonstrated officer potential by her strategic and tactical planning, not to mention her management of the troop. Further, he had no reliable officers in Captains Butkins and

Terrell whose frequent absences interrupted the chain of command. Sweenie's thoughts shifted to the ripple effect the promotions would have within the militia; they will bring us closer together and in so doing change the nature of our relationship to ourselves and to our country. And the media event made of it will call the public attention in a positive and meaningful, but no less dramatic fashion.

"At ease, Troop, I have good news: the following privates are hereby promoted to the rank of corporal," and he ran the list of the erstwhile Pyrates. "Promoted to Sergeant are Adelroy and Legroy Funderbarke, and last but by no means least, Sergeant Stratt is hereby promoted to the rank of Lieutenant. My heartiest congratulations to one and all. Now we must make this event known to the community!"

The ranks just stood there silently gaping; but even the slowest (except Dewit) of them was quick to size up the situation: Sergeant Bitch was a crabby, joyless task master and tough on the eyes, but as Sergeant she had been one of them; now she was—don't say it! And a scramble ensued and in the flash of a redneck rumba they were gone, all except for Dewit, Buster, the Funderbarkes and Lynette, who then marched up to the Commandant and saluted.

"Sir, with this promotion I have decided to take my training here with T.R.A.S.H. and apply it to the United States Army. With your permission, Captain Butkins will drive me to the recruiting office in Ashville."

"Lieutenant, I think that's a splendid idea. You'll make a fine soldier."

In a moment more, it appeared that the entire troop had departed.

Well, any militia is going to see some changes, Sweenie reasoned, you see, we're just ordinary citizens who take up the call. Besides, I've still got a few, my chief scout and his brother. The twin Funderbarke boys had organized a game of pin-the-tail-on-the-donkey, lining up a blindfolded Dewit with a chained-up Reagan. Sweenie left them and caught a lift into town with his departing officer corps and as they drove away Dewit was headed for the tree line, the paper tail in his outstretched hand.

Merle Terrell emerged from the woods at dusk and finding the house empty, he sat his horse on the front sidewalk and whittled a stick. A car pulled into the driveway and a man got out.

"Hello Sir, my name is Aaron Salmon. Is Mr. Sweenie home?" Terrell didn't appear to have heard him as the penknife scratched and brush crickets out-chirped others.

"Uh, if I'm not bothering you, sir, I have great news to share with this militia group about the future of The Republic of Pee Dee County." Terrell looked upward his long face silhouetted against the violet sky.

"One tenth," he said.

"Yes, sir," and as the two men chatted, Terrell realized that this was his chance. It had been slipping steadily away, as had his confidence in Sweenie's ability to do anything other than talk a good game. In those heady, early days the troop had made an inspiring sight on maneuvers. Well, most of them anyway. They'd set traps, dug trenches, laid wire, and a host of martial duties. But then something changed the tone of his enthusiasm and colored his initial skepticism a shade darker: he'd observed them using slingshots and BB guns on live fire exercises. Just saving their ammo, he had thought at the time. Then one day from the promontory where he like to sit his horse, the problem was concluded: it wasn't ammo. Balloons had been tied to the branches of trees as targets for a fusillade, and when all was set, a single shot was fired from an M-16 and the trooper then hustled it to the next position where another shot was fired, and so on. Terrell was dumbstruck that his Republic's militia had only one rifle! He soon discovered that while his grandson had a carload of guns, he was charging exorbitant rates to lease them, and then for 24 hours only. Couldn't blame him, though, you couldn't be a Terrell unless you was a tightwad. Now, the first good news to come his way in so long made him uncertain how to trust it.

"What's the catch?" he said.

"There's no catch, Mr. Terrell. What I'm telling you is the honest truth, and there's only one problem as I see it."

"What's that?" he said, but thought, I knew it!

"It's uncertain which part of your land is the best to use."

"Salmon, that ain't a problem a tall," and he extracted a letter from an inside pocket and handed it across, and Aaron read the latest DOT missive by the light of Terrell's Zippo.

"Now, young man, what you got to do is keep your mouth shut. I still need Sweenie and his bunch, for a little while, anyway. He hears about this and the whole deal goes down the toilet." They shook hands. Aaron drove into town and booked a motel room for the night, too excited to drive home. He called his wife and gave her the news. Then he went out to find a restaurant, hopefully one that served champagne.

~ ~ ~

For a man not easily ruffled, L.D. McKee was so disturbed by the anonymous call that suggested he hot foot it to cooler climes, he couldn't remain seated. He poured another drink, but then set it down. He dashed to the bedroom and filled two suitcases. Next, he emptied the wall safe and dumped his wife's jewelry on top of it, and was contemplating the silverware too, when the thought of the sword stopped him cold. If the shit hits the fan, the collection will be the first thing they seize: good thing I already sold much the elder Poe a fake, but that sword is mine!

He called his wife at the neighbors and told her he'd be there in ten minutes; they were going out. What else: empty the account at the ATM. When the phone rang, he jumped. He gulped some of his drink and picked up. Silence. He grabbed the bags and ran to the car as the phone rang again. He cursed a blue streak waiting for his wife. That sword is mine, damn it. As he turned the corner, he passed his brother going the other way and made a U-turn and caught Shell in the driveway. They spoke between the idling cars.

"Ty, what's up?"

"I'm glad I caught you. They were doing yard work today. Dad left a rake on the grass and Mom tripped over it and broke her hip; at her age—"

"She's all right?"

"Well, no, she's not. If we show up and stand by her, you know, it will mean a lot." L.D. sighed.

"She's worried now, thinks it was her own fault. We can't allow her to sink like that," added Shell. L.D. calculated.

"I'll meet you at the hospital."

"Well sure, of course," said Shell, "is everything all right?"

"Everything's fine," he said, and got back in his car. The two pair of headlights stabbed the darkness in opposite directions. L.D. drove aimlessly; he wanted to flee and aimed the car toward the interstate until his conscience got the better of him and he made a U-turn.

L.D cruised past the hospital. He went around the block and again used the speed bumps to allow him to case the front entrance and approaches.

"Look out!" cried Daisy, and he just missed an old man with a cane.

"What in the world is the matter, Leutius?"

"Looking for Ty," he said, as he went around the block again.

"He's supposed to meet me out front."

"Probably he's with Millie, as we should be."

This time he double-parked at the entrance, but soon a hospital security vehicle pulled in behind him and flashed its lights. As he drove away, he noted police officers in the entryway.

"Look honey, run in and when you see him come back out and wave." Daisy got out of the car and he went around the block again. This time he saw the car. Alright, Shell's here, but where?

Daisy found her brother-in-law sitting on a bench near the large front window. He looked up.

"Where's L.D.?"

"What in the world is going on?"

"Well, uh, these gentlemen would like to speak to him."

"He's—he wants me to wave to him," she said to her brother-in-law and two men on either side of him who were interested in the conversation. One of them produced a leather wallet. The other man was on his cell phone.

"Let's go wave to him, Daisy," said Shell, steering her by the elbow.

"Something's wrong," said L.D. as he left the entranceway and strode back to his car, lost in thought as the ambulance drew closer. He pulled to the side to let it pass, but it wasn't an ambulance, and the officer said,

Leutius Damocles McKee and then read him his rights, and he felt that his precious sword had plummeted from on high and pierced him to the heart.

6

Randal and Missy spent the next several weeks in his bedroom at Elmer's house, rarely getting up before noon, and then only to play with Otis Rose or to make waffles, the post-coital inaugural meal of entanglement.

"I like the way they look like a big fly swatter," she said one afternoon as he ladled out blueberry preserves, running a temperature from ginger fever.

"And the berries are like dead flies." She bolted from the table. "OH! That's just *gross* Randal Poe! You make me sick!"

Randal would perforce remember that door slam as denouement.

"Damn!" he looked at Otis who sat on Buster's chair, a fur ball with a tongue. "It wasn't that bad, was it?" The dog replied in a fit of yelping. For the rest of the day Missy wouldn't speak to him, and he was made to knock and ask for his toothbrush; that night he had to sleep on the couch and was thus positioned to witness the morning's events, rising to see Eddie Terrell packing his car, but in time that stood still just then, poised between sleep and dreams, as an observer detached, not unlike when he ate with his parents and they spoke about him in the third person; when he awoke from this spell, Missy was Eddie's girlfriend and the two of them were gone.

"Look to the bright side," said Buster, who sat on the coffee table polishing his scalp with a pair of boxer shorts, "she didn't give you the clap as a going away present."

"You mean crabs," said Elmer, as he washed down pork rinds with beer, and without another thought, "that's what she gave me."

Abandoned by some vagary of love, Randal had lusted upon its fringe, seeking some measure without plumbing its varied depths, and though it seemed possible such a feat could be accomplished through sanguinary sex, he had lost there as well. His thoughts flashed on his father and how perhaps love was an understudy waiting in the wings for the hero to trip and take a nosedive, center left.

The next morning after Elmer had gone to work and before Buster was yet awake, Randal loaded his few possessions into Peaches and set off for the mountains, but first he had several stops to make. He was surprised to find the door open and no one at home, though he caught a faded whiff of his mother's perfume, that lilac miasma that made his skin crawl. It was spooky, and he felt much like he always had, an intruder, roughly sensing that it was not just his dad, the focal point of his disillusion, who'd always made him feel like an overstaying guest, and he recalled how seldom they were home together, when one or the other wasn't glad handing at the country club, hosting an event at Carolingian or off in a wing of the manse, plastered.

He emptied the liquor cabinet in the living room as well as the one in the study, but the kitchen he knew held only Scuppernong, a wine of the bilges it seemed to say, and what did that tell you, and had reached the foot of the basement steps and flicked on the light when a figure leaped out, but a raised arm stopped the Whiffle bat and the two of them withstood the shock of the moment, Randal with an out-of-whack sense of huh and Matilda with Oh thank god on her face before she dropped the bat and offered a tentative, fretful hug.

Randal broke her feeble link to sit on the bottom step. She sank beside him, grabbing his legs.

"Randal, I—" and the rest was muffled in sobs.

"Mom, don't, it's okay just don't, look it's—"

"I'm gone… live here anymore… beat me." He'd never seen her like this and it scared him. She was always so steely, and he had no bearing, no way to gauge; their interaction had ever been managed by booze, yet he blamed himself for relegating her to shadow status, to some stylized zombie pretention, but even so, he didn't know her, didn't know how to talk to her, and his thoughts shifted to Elmer and to Sweenie, out there where tomorrow's answer is in the wind.

"Honey, I have been errant, I know… my failing, but allow me the chance to make it up to you; please dear, I *need* my family." Her sincerity was dissimulated by tone, what to him mimicked the annual Yuletide mp3 sent to relatives, the cardboard cutouts, and he dodged.

"What's all that stuff over there?"

"I came here to destroy his booze locker."

"Came… mom, what's going on?"

"He was a really sweet guy, but this… Randal, I need you to be with me."

"Sweet isn't a word I'd link to him," said Randal, as they walked to the stacked cases of beer and an odd assortment of bottles, casks, and demijohns. "Well, he can have me, or he can have *this*," she said, uncapping a bottle of Gin and taking a swig, then another, and Randal witnessed the common refrain unfold, how he was erased from the equation as she walked past him without a glance and climbed the stairs. It took him less than ten minutes to load, and when he was done he went in search of her and thought he caught a whiff of lilac and gin on the back stairs, a red flag mnemonic, but he pressed on into many rooms and at last found her in the sun porch where he stood in the doorway wanting to reach out to her, to lead her away from trouble, but the immensity of the dilemma blocked all thought save for the image of a thermometer as a swizzle stick, so that all he did give to her was Ramseur's contact info and then a halting, tremulous hug that sought to encradle the absent embrace of years, but alas a gulf too wide, and he unwrapped her arms and floated from the room.

When he drove away from Umstead Mills, the truck was crammed with beer, liquor and mementos, and the big yellow motorcycle. Gassing up before he hit the freeway, he sent a text to Mr. Ramseur from his Smart phone which was more of a summary of events than a correspondence, unaware that the journalist already knew how to locate him.

His second stop seemed even riskier, but he had been dying to know what had happened to the Honeycutts and hadn't really pursued this line of thought too far, perhaps because Sweenie had counseled that people who knew too much got disappeared, but what about zillions of pigs? They were certainly smart animals; he idly wondered if swine could be debriefed; science was doing some amazing stuff; he would ask Legroy when he saw him; the scout had an eye and an ear for the arcane.

Driving into Bessboro the first thing he noticed was the air: it smelled like, well, air; he was alert to the implications, and went warily through the gate and as he crested the rise behind the office he took in the scene: it used to be his favorite place because from that vantage point you could see the rows of silver barns that stretched to the horizon; it was the place where you went to behold and marvel at the splendor of industrial pork on the hoof. This day, however, brought no such feelings of the sublime. Instead, they were replaced by the silence and the utter stillness of the now deserted farm. He stood transfixed.

"Hey you!" Startled, Randal jumped, whacking a funny bone.

"Cobb, is that you?"

"Damn, Randal, I thought you was a burglar."

"What would I steal?"

"We got nothin, nothin! Bank shut us down, too." He lit a cigarette, surveyed the farm.

"But… why, why did they take them away?"

"Government says we fucked up," and he went on, listing the accusations and filling in the details, but Randal wasn't listening. The word 'government' had shaken him. My God, can it be?! Much of what Sweenie and the troopers of T.R.A.S.H. had told him he'd taken with a giant grain of salt, for it reeked like so much outlandish bullshit, and it was just across the road at the motel that the Ramseurs had justified his scorn that there were Russian armored divisions on the Yucatan peninsula. Well, the commandant had some of it wrong, probably from listening to Dewit, but what he had correct seemed to be right on the money!

He tuned in Cobb again.

"Next week, my brother Durwood gets out the bughouse."

"Where's your wife?"

"They're both up to Raleigh. Everbody, the whole damn family is broke up."

"I'm really sorry Cobb."

"They got your operation, too."

"But I bought that Ferris wheel with cash," said Randal.

"No, man, Sow Syrup, Pig Parlor; they got it all."

Randal's heart sank like a rock, and he moaned, guessing it had all begun with his environmental hotline phone call. Oh man, you flush your own toilet, but it's not supposed to back up on you.

"Shit on a stick! L.D.'s going to have my ass now, for sure."

"L.D.? That low-down dirty sonofabitch the one got us in this mess," spat Cobb. "I'd shoot his sorry ass if I thought it'd change anything."

They sat on the steps and drank some brew, and Randal learned about his mentor's collaboration with Cobb's unwitting assistance and about bribery and toxic microbes and fish kills and mulled it over and over. What a colossal mess it was. Then he had an idea and rummaged around in Peaches until he found the right box that held the maps to the Republic of 1/10th of PeeDee County; they'd printed hundreds to hand out as souvenirs.

"There's plenty of room for y'all up there and whatever livestock you've got left or can get back, I mean they can't keep 'em forever, right? And I can help out with trucks, probably about all I got left," as a thought struck him, a dawning shot that his investment in the motel and in Bessboro might have gone along with the pigs. Who would stay in the motel now? There would be no more tours, so no more guests, no more ads to attract them, and with no fast food, and no nightclub act, even the Ferris wheel would be useless, the bumper cars empty and silent, and with his outlay on the soft drink also gone, he had little income to make his payments to McKee. Both Randal and Cobb now sat with their heads in their hands; it was really too big a tangle to be grasped in its entirety, and perhaps that had been the spark that ignited Durwood's rampage. Randal could only approach a single filament of the braid at any one time. Each thread carried its own ominous signs, such as why Sow Syrup had been taken away, it wasn't the soft drink that killed a million fish. He was afraid to think beyond these portents for fear of what his own brain might uncover and guessed that this must be what every day was like for Dewit. He would have been a good deal more disturbed if he had known that a warrant had been issued for his arrest.

~ ~ ~

Upon returning the rental truck and grumbling his way through the paperwork, Poe drove somberly home; his grand plan to snare his spawn had gone so far afield as to seem like another dimension, and it pained him to have lost control almost from the outset. After a shower and a change of clothes he still seethed but held himself from ripping the head off the kid from Dominoes. Later he awoke, uncertain of his whereabouts, having fallen asleep in the recliner, the half-eaten pizza on the coffee table in front of the TV. Ordinarily he would surf away from news blather, but tonight, as the cobwebs receded, he was too wasted to care, and listened to kidney stones and apartment fires and lost dogs. It soon ended and was followed by the national news and the lead story was a hoot: a group of tax resistors in the mountains of North Carolina had declared a parcel of land to be a republic, and after hoisting their own flag, they had proclaimed secession from the union. After months of mounting tedium and frustration over the federal government's unwillingness to negotiate or even to recognize their existence, they had taken the only avenue left to them: they opened a theme park.

Poe nearly vaulted out of his chair when the anchor interviewed bands of militiamen, for staring spellbound at the camera as he answered questions and smiled at millions of viewers was his own flesh and misbegotten blood. Then, he got another shock when the camera panned a second individual, a bony galoot in an ill-fitting Uncle Sam uniform. The captioned names appeared at the bottom of the screen, as though he needed to be reminded of who those assholes were. This calls for a drink, he thought, but when he reached into the cabinet, he grabbed air, and when he found his hideaway gone and the riddled reserve in the basement, he ruminated on the only person who ever stole his drink as he drove to the liquor store, but managed not to snarl at the clerk. The next morning, he set out red eyed and made a plan on the go: this time no hair dye, no costumes, no dress rehearsals; this time he'd play it straight; play it by the book; no guess work, no under-cover shenanigans, just get in and get it done and get out.

7

At the first sound of engines and the sighting of strange vehicles through the trees, Commandant Sweenie deployed into action, but almost from the start he grasped that something had gone awry. The reports from his scout told him of machinery disproportionate to the task of carving a swath wide enough to build a road. After a period of twenty-four hours in his command post, he crept stealthily through the brush (see page 17 of the T.R.A.S.H. handbook) to an upwind downgrade overlook and fixed his binoculars on the scene below. He could hardly believe his eyes: the construction crews that had begun to transform the landscape around him were not from the Department of Transportation, whose bright yellow vehicles were recognizable anywhere in North Carolina. Furthermore, they were busy building structures that resembled, no, it couldn't be, bunkers and pillboxes?

When he learned from Chief Scout Legroy what was really going on, he sank into a pit of sorrow and shapeless anger where he wallowed for another twenty-four hours, forlorn amid the missed opportunities of struggle and strike. Then, he and Terrell argued the issue and that of the direction of the troops. It's still a Republic, the old man had stated, and as long as it stayed one there was only one commander. Sweenie was buffaloed. He didn't know whether to attack or retreat, and as a result his orders were clueless and his thrusts ineffective. Terrell had seniority on him, and not only in rank, but also through decades of hidebound cynicism.

"What I can't understand," Sweenie complained, "is how you expect to fight the government this way. First, there'll be regulations, then codes, quotas, and finally, taxes."

"You don't understand, I can see," said Terrell.

"I guess I don't," said Sweenie, shaking his head. They were standing at the railing atop the recently completed Rappelling Tower that overlooked the park's rifle range, the training course, and a section of the new zip line.

"Second, how many Republics are there with "Incorporated" in their names?"

"Just one, so far as I know," said Terrell, proudly. A hawk sailed past the tower, perhaps checking out these strange new birds on their lumber aerie.

"Listen sonny boy, my new adjutant, Salmon, explained it in a way I could understand. I saw the light." Terrell then offered up tidbits of the enterprise. Sweenie turned crimson.

"Damn! You switched sides is what you did!" said Sweenie.

"What about you?" replied Terrell softly, as he looked down his nose at the sniveling camo-clad whiner. "What about the money you gonna get from the cereal, huh? You tellin' me that you're not interested in makin' a pile?"

"It's taxes," bleated Sweenie.

"There's ways around taxes, rich folk do it all the time, and they ain't wear jungle suits."

"But that's—"

"That's the way it is. You can fight two different ways, and I'm too damn old to be runnin' around dodgin' bullets with the likes of the Funderbarkes, them boys ain't right." Terrell left him there and rappelled down the wall like Spiderman's grandfather.

Sweenie then ran through his options. Since his command post was slated to become the parking lot information kiosk (*You Are Here*), and since parking lots always imposed their will on the people, channeling them like lemmings into distant meridians, acres away from the mercantile pulse, by God he would stay at his post and defend it against encroachment. He shambled down the stairs blue but determined and headed off through the wooded hillocks for his HQ at the farmhouse.

Tax Resistors And Southern Heroes had already received an initial check from Capitol Foods for the trademark name, Militia Man Cereal. It promised to be a hot item. Sweenie had even begun his own collection with the prizes to be included in each and every box, but he didn't know how he really felt about it all, he wasn't exactly working for the income. It was more like panhandling than it was punching a clock, or maybe somewhere in between. Then there were taxes. If he played it their way, he wouldn't get all his money. He was then distracted by the arrival of Randal with an armful of mail and then by Dewit, who delivered an unordered wok sized bowl of instant macaroni and cheese, saluted, and marched out. The two of them sat in the living room and ate the pasta in its swampy orange goo as Reagan lay asleep at their feet, twitching and whimpering.

"Uh, we can't use that thing I wrote, you know, that thing with the mermaids."

"Randal, that's the centerpiece, and it's the first issue."

"Well, you know Tarleton Ramseur, the columnist; he says it's plagiarized."

"All the better," said Sweenie.

"I'm going to say no, we can't use it."

"Well, I have got to say that I'm sick and tired of people telling me what I cannot do," declared Sweenie. First the old man and now the kid, they're lining up.

"And what does that columnist have to do with this? We're not writing for him anymore."

"He's kind of like my mentor, and you weren't writing for him, I was." Sweenie ignored the jab as he riffled through the mail, sailing bills and flyers toward the fireplace.

"Well, I'll be damned," said Sweenie. Randal glanced at the envelope.

"Who's it from?"

"Mrs. Daryll Ringo."

"Who's that?" Sweenie scanned the letter.

"Dewit's Mom. This is his lucky day; he gets his name back."

Randal pondered his own sense of identity, how it felt to be a stranger in his own family with that who-he-was in relation-to-his-parents trod under foot and forgotten, and though a surrogate resurrected through the kindness of the Ramseurs had been restored to him, the sense of dignity it attached troubled him because its warmth seemed equally humiliating. Stuffed, he went in search of medicine: a book.

Across the road and up the hill, Legroy and Adelroy marveled at the new machinery installed in the physical plant, which was a squat boxlike structure with a crenellated facade, made to resemble a fort. The motors would run the heating and air-conditioning in all the buildings, as well as the mechanical devices, such as the pop-up metal targets over at the Search and Destroy Range, where for a mere twenty-five bucks a visitor could hunt for the enemy.

They were going to be in charge of all things mechanical. It wouldn't just be cars this time, no sir. There was a motorcycle with a sidecar, two jeeps, a (plywood) tank, snowmobiles, the chair lift, and the list went on. While they would stand to make decent money, they had been strictly forbidden to dismantle anything unless it needed fixing; that was going to be a hard one, given their talent to take something apart and put it back together so quickly that it seemed like sleight of hand.

"We could take old Dewit apart and put him back together too, if he was a machine," explained Adelroy, tapping a box wrench against his forehead.

"Do him a world of good," said Legroy.

"You know what, Dewit got his name back," said Randal, and then told the twins how the woman had seen her son on T.V. when they did that story on the Republic of PeeDee County. She wanted to send him some socks.

"Socks?" said Adelroy.

"Ringo?" said Legroy.

"Dewit don't even know how to tie his shoes, how're socks gonna help?" They went in search of the gentle giant to give him the good news.

8

Dr. Titus Shell was also the recipient of good news that day: His brother was selling his collection. The phone call had been terse and the details sketchy; he knew for sure only that the lot had been seized following McKee's arrest in connection with the environmental disaster down east. As curator of the state's premier history museum, he relished the thought of getting the first bid. Museums would be among the first recipients of the inventory, and item number one was General Shives Poe's dress sword engraved with the name J.E.B. Stuart. Shell had had a moment of fright when shown the report by a colleague, but he'd recovered quickly and stated that it was a replica and that he had sent the collector the photo upon request—and then he had a brainstorm.

After making the necessary phone calls and arranging to inspect the object, he punched the address into his GPS and let the electronic voice guide him. The warehouse sat in a string of similar buildings behind a chain-link fence. Shell flashed his state I.D. at the gate and went inside. While he knew roughly the size of his brother's collection, he wasn't prepared for what he encountered as he passed into the central storage area: ambulance wagons, caissons, tents, furniture, uniforms, flags, cannon, mortars, ramrods, rifles, barrels of minie balls and piles of rotting tack, the traces snaked along the floor. He handed an employee the tag number he'd been given at the receiving desk. The sword lay in a crude wooden box and he lifted the heavy weapon and drew the blade from the scabbard. In the florescent glare it looked alike to his exhibition piece and thinking it through, he saw that there was yet one hurdle to jump. Hurrying back to his office, he deleted the letter L.D. had sent him regarding their arrangement and beneath the Hogville letterhead he typed: 'Dr. Titus Shell is hereby given sole privilege of inspecting and /or making full use of the replica of the Poe sword etcetera if ever the need should arise,' and he then predated it, looked it over, added an encomium after his title, and satisfied it would do, scrawled his brother's signature and printed two copies and folded one into his coat pocket. With the help of a technician, the display sword was swaddled in bubble wrap and in a moment, elapsed time in abeyance, he was back at the impound yard and hedging the truth as he explained the situation to the manager of the facility. Before long he had the two swords laid out, side by side, and saw what L.D. would also have appreciated: the clear differences between the replica and the genuine item. The General's initials on the hilt were of a finer gilt, and the artwork on the ricasso was immaculate, the detailing superb. The scabbard too was different, for on the solid brass frog stud was stamped a tiny rebel flag. He lowered the loupe and thought about the series of events that led to his brother's sale to the senior Poe of the unadorned battle cutlass. Who'd been the more deceitful? Then there was the Poe kid. What an awful mess, but it would no longer cook his own goose. Rewrapping one blade and seating the other back in the box, he noted the guard had his nose in a newspaper, and handing in his pass at the receiving desk he trod so lightly from the warehouse that he seemed to float. The letter had been wholly unnecessary.

~ ~ ~

The Ramseurs had also seen the newscast about the theme park, and the following day Tarleton got wind of the arrest of L.D. McKee, and of his collection of Civil War artifacts, one item of which had for a brief time sat upon his desk. After several attempts, he got through to the museum curator.

"Why Mr. Ramseur, this is a pleasure indeed. How may I help you?"

"I was wondering what you could tell me about your relations with the Poe family."

After a protracted silence the curator replied:

"They are a most unsavory lot."

"Can you be more specific, sir? I am primarily concerned about the son, although the father does bear watching."

"He should be watched by men in white coats," said Shell. He then reminded Ramseur about Poe's visit to the museum and how the diminutive author had gone berserk, attacked him.

"As I understand it now," Shell continued, "the boy sold a fake of his father's heirloom to a private collector but sold the original to us, and I'd greatly appreciate it if you kept that well under your hat; we don't seek adverse publicity."

"You needn't worry, sir. I have no desire to tarnish this fine institution," said Tarleton.

"Apparently, the boy was also selling the family estate, piece by piece," said Shell.

"I'm surprised he'd have title," said Tarleton.

"Oh no, I meant his grandfather's accoutrements, although he has been forging his father's signature, so title wouldn't mean a whole lot to whoever owned that house and a rather large chunk of land that the elder, that disturbed man, has used as collateral for his bail. The only reason I know this is—"

"Excuse me, sir, would you know the location of that land? It may be important."

"Well, I believe it's up in the mountains near Ashville," and it dawned on Tarleton that he knew right where it was, and following the pleasantries required to disengage from banter, he called his wife as he headed for the door.

"Sweet, Poe's headed for the hills!"

"Which one is, Tarl?"

"Perhaps both, and gosh darned it turns out to be a place we've been to before, rife with snake oil and fuzzy dice."

"I think I know where you mean, B.J. And we're going back, aren't we, hon?"

"You bet your bat cave we are."

"Then we'll be going with a guest. Poe's estranged wife has also been hunting for her son. We have been talking and she has asked for our help to put her in touch with her family. She's in a room at the Sheraton."

"Okay sweetkins, thank you, we'll pick her up on our way out of town. Now, here's what we need."

While the Ramseurs pondered the folly of revenge, the Honeycutts were bent upon it. As dusk melted into darkness, they parked their trucks and waited. The plan they'd hatched for this night had as its origin the day the bank foreclosed on their loan, following the seizure of their farm which for generations had been the family homestead where strong inbred community ties had matured through the management of the spread, but now it was all gone. "The hell it is," thundered Durwood, as he paced in his hospital bathrobe.

Gladys too, in her own way, had come out of the doldrums over Doodlebug and Tinkerbell and gotten feisty and furious; she and her sister had been the instrument of raising the spirits of the rest of the clan. Once Betty's husband had been released into her custody, pending trial for assault on fourteen law enforcement officers, two agriculture agents, a news photographer and a bystander, the two galvanized the misbegotten family into a force to be reckoned with.

Two pick-up trucks came out of the drive, their taillights disappearing around the bend. Employees headed home, and Dale counted one thousand twenty times and then flashed the tail lights signal to move out from his, the lead vehicle. Though it'd been but a couple days shy of a month that he'd worked there, it was long enough to have learned the layout, and he silently thanked Randal's trucking company as the line of them, headlights off, moved as quietly as big rigs could into the heart of the Agricultural Research Station.

The night manager turned up the volume when they put on the Super Grit Cowboy Band. With his feet up on the shelf behind the desk, hands laced behind his head he digested his supper and got down with the dudes, and while he thought he heard a car door, when nobody came in, he didn't pay it any mind. Besides, the deejay had just promised Waylon.

The loading went without a hitch though the squealing gave a jittery Gladys the giggles. Heck with it, what can they do to us they ain't already done, she reasoned.

Betty was heard to remark, "is these are hogs?" Some had metal plates protruding from their heads; many of them seemed blind; countless others cast about with smoldering eyes.

"Hogs is hogs," whispered Gladys, confident of a Tinkerbell reunion. Soon Dale came down the line, made sure everybody knew what to do, though they'd been over it a hundred times, and they crept off into the night. When her truck snagged a fence and lurched, a determined Gladys gripped the wheel and put the hammer down. The manager was in the john when he heard someone cutting sheet metal. The hell was that? But he couldn't investigate until he'd finished his trip on the porcelain bus. What he found, at last, was thirty feet of fencing ripped from the ground and strewn down the road, but no sign of anything or anyone, and he wondered if it hadn't been aliens, and scanned the heavens for mysterious lights as he hustled wayward pigs. By the time he called the Sheriff, the Honeycutt convoy was moving inexorably toward its destination, a place, Dale had assured them, that no one would think to look.

"We can start up again out there."

~ ~ ~

Everett Poe had the surprise of his life as he drove onto his land. Where there had been a large overgrown field was now a freshly paved and striped parking lot. It hadn't been too long ago that he'd stood there arguing with that goat, Terrell. What has that sonofabitch done? They got a convention center here, got a Target? He couldn't believe his eyes, and soon got directions from a construction worker on where to find the old man. I'll deal with these militants later. Driving the rutted, washed- out dirt road, he gunned along for what seemed like miles then fishtailing when he slid through a hairpin turn and into a pond sized chuckhole and before he could accelerate the Cadillac was stuck fast, muddy water oozing under the doors. He tried reverse. He tried rocking it. He tried cursing out loud. Finally, he tried the whiskey that he'd bought in town. Leaning on the horn, he let it rip. Another snort of the bourbon and he gave the horn a good five minutes, cranking Tchaikovsky to mask it but when all he heard was the twittering woods and birds between his curses, he determined to leap from the car to dry ground. Huffing to clamber out the window he had just gained the roof when a pack of snarling dogs, must have been a dozen, surrounded the puddle, and when two surged through the murk and leaped to the hood he swung the bottle as he backed away; the windshield was his only defense, as their claws couldn't grip the glass, but they leapt and snarled, lips curled in bloodlust and it was from the brougham roof that Poe began to yell, giving it everything he was worth.

Merle Terrell tried on his new suit. They call it a costume they want, but I think this is damn nice. Somewhere he'd heard it called a tuxedo but couldn't trace the memory. Next, he tried the top hat, turning in front of the mirror and adjusting the rake when he heard a car horn up the road a piece. Damn fool, one a

Salmon's boys, a dime get chew a dollar. The horn came again. A hunter out a season, take my deer! He fingered the middle button, and then buttoned it again. The horn continued to blare, as he turned sideways to admire his ninety-year-old flat stomach: Never so much as a crease. The mirror smiled but the honking continued unending, unbearable. Within minutes he was striding through the woods with his rifle.

Well, I'll be a suck-egg dog, if it ain't that pint-size pecker head. He stood in brambles and watched Poe yell. I'm put one right through your sorry ass, but as he raised the rifle a better idea hit and he retraced his steps, some of the dogs trailing behind. Twenty minutes later he left his horse with Legroy with instructions that it was in good health and not to take it apart. "It's a horse. Be back in a while," and he drove off in the park's latest acquisition.

Poe had found a different kind of hoarse, and settled down to nursing it with the whiskey, as the dogs, no longer frantic to shred him, settled down to a siege. He drank a while and smoked a cigar and then thought that he heard an engine somewhere off behind the growling. Wait! There it was again! Now he was sure of it, a truck, about fucking time! He was patting his pockets for another cigar when the half-track bounded through the curve and ploughed into the Caddy. The impact knocked Poe from the roof where he sprawled on the hood glaring back at the Army truck that surged his car along through cathedral trees and in building fear a cackling laughter followed him as the car fell away and he tumbled into space.

Poe awoke beside the upturned car, wheels caked in mud. As he lay there fighting for breath, a man's face appeared well above him laughing hard and hearty and Poe turned to the oozing hulk beside him: Come not between the dragon grapes of wrath… but when he came to again, he wondered who spoke the lines, and they weren't right, there was, there was something off-angle, and he lay still in his mud bed and tried to clear his head from a crazy dream! Uncle Sam had stood over him yelling: I Want You; the spoken lines merged and confused, and he dozed and listened to birds high up, all around him, high above, and he lay quite still while listening and checking for broken bones and then wobbled to his feet, ankle deep in bog and covered in muck. I got to get out of this. He took a step and fell, and tried again, vision blurred with pain he noticed his car: funny, Caddy, downside up… grease up… sky up… Army, what's at, got tracks… dogs… whiskey… Uncle Sam, cigar… need cigar. He fell again and moaned, get, get out of here; oh, Matilda dear, do help your daddy. Beside him he saw the cutlass, brought along to whip his son with the flat of the blade, but though he couldn't connect its presence it made a handy crutch to help him to his feet.

~ ~ ~

Randal filled the ice chest with food and carried it to his truck. He'd been manning the HQ when the Funderbarkes made supply runs; it was a good arrangement. There were phone calls and stuff, and he got to play at being a big shot again, like L.D. except that… well skirting his brief sojourn as entrepreneur this reminded him of the Civil War reenactment events: ketchup vendors had some status; it's better to be the boss. This was way different, oh yeah. That kind of running around in the woods is just stupid, though he hadn't told Sweenie. At least with the Civil War stuff you had an obvious foe. Here the only enemy is deer ticks and you can't fight them, but they can sure kill you. Sweenie can get out there if he wants, but I'm not getting ants up my crack for any reason. The phone rang. It was a message for Sweenie and there was no one else to deliver it. But he knew that a real boss was stand up, so he hiked once again into the woods.

It seemed to Sweenie that he himself had become a different person, assumed a new command, almost. Since he'd learned of the park, he had accused Mr. Terrell of selling out and had vowed to fight on and further, claimed he would prevent development of the Republic or die trying. Randal contemplated the hackneyed situation as he made his way through the trees. Commandant of what, he's got Legroy part-time, Adelroy hardly at all, a three-legged dog with mange, and Dewit; a couple of Boy Scouts could kick his ass. If this was a Chickamauga skirmish it might be different, but the only Yankee anywhere close to the Republic is that guy Salmon, and he lives in Richmond. When he arrived at the outpost, Sweenie told him to hold the fort while he took care of the message.

That had been the day before, or was it two, and Randal straggled back to the farmhouse, dirty and tired. At last, he came out of the shower feeling like a million bucks and got a spoonful of peanut butter, rolling it and savoring this treat when the phone rang. Last time I answered it I had to spend three days behind barbed wire with Dewit!

"Speak to Randal Poe."

"Cobb?"

"Hey, bud, listen, gimme directions again to your place: we up here with a load your old pals." The Honeycutts had driven west from the sand hills into the mountains, but not in convoy for Dale/Cobb had been crafty in his planning. Each truck took a different route to Bluff, yet they had arrived at the Republic of 1/10th of PeeDee County in tandem, and parked nose to tail along the road beside the T.R.A.S.H. headquarters. Randal greeted them on the porch where they slapped backs and shook hands all around and after beers made the rounds, they went to check out the six rigs. Man, Legroy would have a field day if he saw all these trucks just sitting here. Cobb leaned against a trailer, snouts poking through the slats, eyeing him. "We broke 'em out, didn't claim a life, and we're here, man." After they had spoken further about the farm and its deliverance, he further said: "We got us a problem. We covered every detail save one. We got no feed, and they're half crazed anyhow. Just look at 'em."

"Will they eat MREs?"

"They'll eat *anything* about now." Randal got them settled in the farmhouse, and he cracked a beer and sat on the porch and considered the hogs, twice stolen and busted out of jail; now there's a cause for Sweenie, far nobler than parking lots. He went off to find the embittered commander, who kept a cache of emergency supplies hidden in a cave.

Merle Terrell paced in front of the ticket booth as painters applied the finishing touches: the work was mostly done and now all they needed were customers. Salmon had assured him that everything was fine; their ad-campaign would draw the crowds. He needn't worry. Again, he looked at his reflection as he passed the front door. Damn sure is a handsome devil. He didn't much care for the red and white striped pants, but the blue tuxedo, red four-in- hand, and blue and white star-banded stovepipe hat was right fancy. He combed out his goatee, grown especially for the role, and jabbed his index finger at his own reflection.

"I Want You," he said. Then he remembered that he wasn't supposed to lean forward. He tried again. "I Want You." Salmon had introduced him to an acting coach hired from the North Carolina School of the Arts in Winston-Salem who had brought out of him the iconic figure like he'd been hiding in there for decades. He'd been given a well-thumbed copy of a book, *Masque and Tasque*, to help him polish the fine points of his new craft. Though he had never admitted to being a book reader, he'd found enjoyment!

As he practiced beneath the archway entrance to the Tax Resistors and Southern Heroes Park a car pulled in and three people got out. He was elated that word had spread so quickly and he strode toward their first customers, one of them a woman dark as a Cherokee and said: "I Want You—to visit our park."

"I'm charmed, Uncle Sam, you're one of my idols," said Matilda, and kissed him on the cheek. Terrell nearly peed himself.

"We would love to visit your park, but we're looking for someone, perhaps you can help us."

Thrown off by the unexpected, for a moment he didn't respond. "Do what I can."

Matilda produced a photograph of her husband.

"You kin?" he said.

"I'm his wife," said Matilda.

Damn, another one, thought Terrell, then struck by the realization of who Randal likely was.

"Never seen him before, but you follow this road on a way you see a house on down there, ask them, you look for a big ole white flag with purple letters."

They talked it over and decided that Matilda would take the car down to the house while the Ramseurs remained at the park. As she drove away, Uncle Sam again approached: "I Want You—to buy tickets!"

~ ~ ~

"Dewit, I tole you for a hundred times the Woolybooger don't ever leave the bottom on account he got nowhere else to go."

"But Scout, I seen him!"

"No, you ain't."

"Scout, down below where the General got his road!"

"Listen, the Woolybooger don't let his self be seen, musta been your reflection in one them puddles. Like I said before, it don't ever leave."

"Why?" Legroy felt himself about to slide in deeper, and he fixed the trembling giant with a knowing stare.

"Because it got two left feet."

"Two feet on the left? What's it got on the right?"

"Two arms."

Dewit whistled.

"Now Dewit, listen up, imagine you had two left feet and two right arms, would you wanna leave the trailer park?" They had been sitting on the giant jackboots of the Militia Man statue just inside the front gate, where visitors encounter the mammoth icon of freedom and so take a pic and then buy tickets from Uncle Sam. A couple approached, but Legroy sensed questions and scooted away.

"Excuse me, we're looking for this guy who may have been here recently," said Tarleton, offering a picture. The man leaped to his feet screaming and raced off.

"What was that he yelled? asked Carolotta.

"I didn't catch it, wooly-something" said Tarleton. "Let's look around some more, shall we?" They strolled over to a firing range where for two dollars one could select from a rack of pellet-firing machine guns and blaze away at metal pop-up targets emblazoned with slogans such as *One World Government, Black Helicopters, 1040EZ,* and more. From behind the structure, they overlooked the construction in progress as a squad of hardhats put the finishing touches on a kiosk, while at another a man in camouflage fatigues and a steel pot scribbled.

Sweenie had settled into his command post for yet another vigilant afternoon after a morning spent trying out combinations of camo paint on Reagan who added a patina of mulch by rolling in the underbrush. Now he sat back with pen and paper, (his digital tablet, bought from cereal proceeds, was charging) to continue his manifesto.

He'd been writing since the arrival of this monstrosity, this park, and by gum, he wasn't going to give up the lower parking lot without a fight, a point made abundantly clear to that Quisling, Terrell: "Let them come, I'll soon have an entire battalion posted there," referring to an arrangement worked out with the Honeycutts. Ringed as it was with a berm, the lot would make an ideal pen for the swine, but he was uncertain of the wording: perhaps 'enemy vehicle park' or 'bogey collection point,' but found himself doodling in the margin when he caught the first grunts of his new recruits. He put down his pen, picked up his rifle and helmet and marched off to take command.

After helping the Honeycutts herd their charges with the use of park ATVs, Randal lent them the use of Peaches so they could pick up groceries in town, and he had just seen them off. He stood arms akimbo by the livestock trucks thinking about the hogs and that the berm was too low to corral them for long, some already heading for the woods, and what to do about it when a car he recognized rounded the curve, and a hundred yards behind it a fleet of vans emerged with flashing lights, but it was the driver of the car pulled up beside him then that had his attention: he couldn't get his head around the oddity of it.

"Mom! What're you *doing* here?"

"Randal—son, we need to start over." Matilda reached for him across the seat.

"Mom, I—"

"No, we, we—"

"Don't you see? I'm done with thumbscrew rules!"

"Son, you are all I have—"

"His side, you always take—"

"After what I've been through!" It was Matilda's turn to be taken aback. "We need each other to work it out." Hesitant, Randal folded his arms on the door frame as she told him of her own trials with Everett, and he began to see her as though for the first time, had sensed at it when they'd met in the basement, and randomly in memory, less a figurehead. She even looked different, not the stylized mom-type version of his dad's other half, but a real person. In that moment Randal fell in love.

"Please dear, I haven't been the best parent, but I aim to change; we can't just run away." Images swarmed of their reading together in the portico, canoeing at the lake, picnics on the grass beneath the side yard magnolia, now suffused in a golden sepia, t'was love that opened the door to climb in when he was grabbed from behind, wrestled to the ground, handcuffed, read his rights, and marched off between rows of assembling uniformed officials and others disgorging from a caravan of trucks and media vehicles.

~ ~ ~

Legroy had disassembled and fine-tuned various gadgets all morning. Now he was at work on a cotton candy machine. When he turned it on, he thought he heard pigs, so he unplugged it and took it apart again. His walkie-talkie buzzed.

"Legroy, you got that 24?" asked his brother.

"Where you at?"

"Don't matter, you got that 24?"

"Yup, but you want it, come git it." Adelroy walked in just then.

"Where was you at?"

"In the ring toss," said his smiling brother.

"Listen, tell me you hear pigs I turn this on." As Legroy flipped the switch they were engulfed in a swarm of frenzied animals and after yanking free his pinkie snipped to the bone, Adelroy leaped onto the counter, followed by his brother.

On the promontory at the base of the flagpole the Ramseurs stood and watched with mounting amazement how a pretty day was mutated by stampeding swine that had materialized from out of nowhere. There was something dreadfully wrong with this scene but the Ramseurs weren't going to wait around to find out and away they flew mere steps ahead of a frothing leviathan as they reached the ladder to the rappelling tower and hoisted themselves up; from the top the view was stunning: rampaging pigs at the compass points like a cloven plague of locusts devoured everything in sight and as construction workers fled in all directions two figures were seen flailing, one of them distant and then the nearest broke free and zigzagged in their direction.

Sweenie had been rehearsing a set of oinks he thought might be useful for addressing raw recruits when the stampede knocked him off his feet and he lost his rifle and then a squealing devil gouged his head and his flailing hands were clamped and gnawed until rage powered him up and he made a howling beeline toward the tower where in its bathroom he found to his horror that he was missing most of his ears, part of his nose, and three fingers. Semaphore in manner, he wound towels about himself and around his head like a turban before dashing back out, beneath the Ramseurs who noted below a man with a bloody face scoot. Through the trees the other man, much further away, seemed to dance about, flail, and dance again. Soon they lost sight of him just as the first man reemerged wearing a red and white mask and who ran and dodged and leaped and ducked into another building, only to appear a moment later with a bun of pink hair. Sweenie had raced from the bathroom and aimed for the gate when he was broadsided by hog phalanx, but he kept his feet and vaulted the counter of the confectionery shop where his momentum carried him head first into the cotton candy machine, to which Legroy was clinging for dear life. Eventually he made it to the gate and a Jeep, his head a turban-like mess of soggy red paper towels, melted pink confectionary, and tears, as he drove toward a circus of bayonets on the county road.

Everett Poe had been dusting the dried mud from his body and removing leaves and twigs from his hair when the big man who'd run screaming from him earlier reappeared and hollered WOOLYBOOGER behind a lattice of fingers and raced off into the brush. This whole place is fucking crazy. I get bushwhacked by Uncle Sam, drowned in mud, then out of that stink hole into a loony-bin stocked for World War III.

He had taken what he needed from stacked crates in a cave and made his way to a stump where he sat gurgling pilfered whiskey. Coming into himself again he was focusing on finding a way out when his ear caught something big and awful tearing through the woods. As he rose to his feet, he was enveloped in a swirling mass of hellacious hogs that ripped and gnashed and tore. He cried out, but the only creature to hear him was shaking him by the throat, and he vanished beneath the fetid mulch that carpeted the forest floor.

~ ~ ~

Two months and two weeks later, a group of friends gathered beneath the spreading limbs of a giant Pin Oak in the yard of the Ramseur home and relaxed in Adirondack chairs.

"Well, Randal, how do you feel, having been chewed up by the system and spit out?" asked Tarleton.

"I'm sure that's not a fair question," said Matilda, "after all that's happened."

"S'okay mom… well sir, first off, I found a home; I got home at last. But I still feel pretty bad for misleading you, but I'd had my heart dead set on journalism; it nearly broke when I didn't make it to Carolingian. So, I just followed through with it anyway and got my start. Once I had name recognition, I sold articles to papers across the state."

"Well, what I meant was your little set-to with the law."

"Ah, sometimes you have to break the rules to get anywhere, uh, but not laws of course, but you know I didn't really break any, just got mixed up with the wrong people, and focused on writing, you know, I wasn't paying too much attention."

"I believe the museum would disagree with that assessment. You swindled them after all, and it harkens a sadder tale: they were planning a larger exhibit with the sabre as the centerpiece of an interactive display on the life and times of your ancestor; it would have been a restoration from the dusk of obscurity to the rosy light of a new dawn, and for the city of Raleigh as well, but not anymore; they have pulled it down," said Tarelton.

"It seems like they could have played on the media hype and used it to their advantage."

"That isn't the way it works my boy; imagine a world in which we champion the feckless, award the maladroit, but your unprompted apology certainly didn't hurt."

"What he did" added Matilda, "was invent a new journalism: create the situation and then tell its story."

"But it's an ethical tangle, a veritable linguini of principles," said Carolotta.

"Is it? A new paradigm dawns," said Matilda, her nose up, as Randal drifted, thinking of L.D. cooling his heels at the Correctional Center in Butner; and of the Honeycutt clan, lionized in the press as Machiavellian underdogs; and of Coleman, who had asked him to get him Tarleton Ramseur's autograph.

"Anything in particular?"

"Well, he used to be a writer, but he lost the fingers on his writing hand."

"Ah, this would be that militia fellow."

"He was lucky he survived."

"From what I know of him, perhaps he's generally unlucky," said Tarleton.

"Luckier than dad, though."

Sheriff's deputies combing the scene found Poe's fingerprints on his Cadillac, a whiskey bottle, and the hilt of a broken vintage sword uncovered near the camo-painted paw of a large dog.

"Wasn't there also another fellow who went missing?" Carolotta asked.

"Yeah, Dewit, he ran off into the swamp that day and just disappeared." Randal recalled how he and Legroy and Adelroy stood at the cliff edge overlooking that vast and spooky bottomland, calling out:

"Ringo!"

"Hey Ringo!"

"Heeeey Riiingggoooo!" And all they heard was the echo of their voices pealing off the distant ridges. Dewit had vanished and would in time become a legend.

"You know what got him," said Legroy.

"I don't even wanna think about it," said Adelroy.

"Your name Randal?"

"My name is Mr. Funderbarke to you, boy."

"Shoot, my daddy wouldn't let you in his family," and on they went as Randal strolled away through the sun-dappled woods, suffused in the aroma of decaying mulch, an odor he would ever associate with the summer he lost his dad but found his mom and began a life in journalism.

The End

About the Author

Other than a brief stint at Naropa Institute to study poetry with luminaries of the Age, Steven Mooney was for twenty years an unskilled blue-collar laborer earning just enough money for the books he devoured across the breadth of world literature. Tiring of the shanty life at thirty-eight, he ventured to college to earn a B.A. in English at the University of North Carolina, and an M.A. in Education from East Carolina University where he encountered ESL.

For the next twenty years he taught English in Central America, The Far East, and the Middle East, then retired to the Pacific Northwest, USA, where he lives with his wife. He is the author of *In Cellophane of Time, Poems 1973-1987*; *Kottke Ouevre Skookum, 6 and 12-string ears, Vignettes 1970-2019*; and the comic literary novels: *Cutlass Wonders*, *The Ageless of Aquarius*, and *Chronicle of an English Morpheme Addict* published under the series title: *A Measure of Poe & Three Quarters* (2020), and *Gunited States* (2023), a free & lyric verse critique of gun culture.

www.ingramcontent.com/pod-product-compliance
Lightning Source LLC
LaVergne TN
LVHW050956080826
845145LV00009B/2325
* 9 7 8 1 7 3 4 5 3 5 6 6 2 *